mOR

Blackpool Council

BUILDING A BETTER COMMUNITY FOR ALL

Please return/renew this item
by the last date shown.
Books may also be renewed by
phone or the Internet.

Tel: 012

www.blac

GW00775788

DEAD SECRET

Criminologist Felix Heron and his wife, Thelma, investigate Sir Percival Trench's death on the hunting field. The inquest's verdict is that it was an accident, but his fiancée thinks otherwise. The case becomes increasingly complex, not least when it appears that Sir Percival's fortune of two hundred and twenty thousand pounds has vanished. Then, when the dead body of a 'grass' is found hanging on a tree — Heron has plenty to work on before finding an unexpected solution.

GERALD VERNER

DEAD SECRET

Complete and Unabridged

LINFORD
Leicester

First published in Great Britain

First Linford Edition
published 2011

British Library CIP Data

Verner, Gerald.
    Dead secret. - - (Linford mystery library)
    1. Criminologists- -Fiction. 2. Nobility- -
    Crimes against- -Fiction. 3. Informers- -
    Crimes against- -Fiction. 4. Murder- -
    Investigation- -Fiction. 5. Detective and
    mystery stories. 6. Large type books.
    I. Title II. Series
    823.9′12–dc22

    ISBN 978-1-4448-0899-5

Published by
F. A. Thorpe (Publishing)
Anstey, Leicestershire

Set by Words & Graphics Ltd.
Anstey, Leicestershire
Printed and bound in Great Britain by
T. J. International Ltd., Padstow, Cornwall

This book is printed on acid-free paper

1

1

Charles Rayner sat at the big, littered writing-table in his study at Trencham Close, writing busily. His pen travelled swiftly over the paper, covering it with the huge, sprawling calligraphy for which he was noted.

Everything about Rayner was huge, his height, the breadth of his shoulders, his great hands, and large but well-shaped head. His face was deeply tanned in spite of the bad summer that year, for it was a legacy of years spent beneath a blazing sun. He was sixty and looked forty-five, virile, and with scarcely a wrinkle on his smooth skin.

The room in which he was trying to catch up with his correspondence, he loathed writing letters, was high-ceilinged with every inch of the wall space covered with book-shelves, housing a collection that must have run into thousands. A deep golden-brown carpet covered the floor, toning with the hide of the easy chairs that stood before the wide, open fireplace in which a cheerful fire was burning.

Over the fireplace, on the only portion of the wall not given over to bookshelves, hung a large oil-painting in a massive gilt frame. It was the painting of a man in lace and ruffles who gazed out of the canvas with a perpetual sneer on his thin-lipped mouth.

Ever since Rayner had come in possession of the house he had wondered who this unprepossessing individual might be and had come to the conclusion, since it had no connection with the man from whom he had bought the house, lock, stock and barrel, that it must have been picked up at a sale somewhere. He had the word of Stukes, the old butler, whom he had taken over with the estate, that the painting did not represent any member of the family.

Stukes had been with the Trench family for years and years. When Sir Percival Trench had died as the result of a hunting accident and the house had been put up for sale, Stukes had been going to retire. It was only after a great deal of argument that Rayner had persuaded him to stay. Butlers were things of the past and he reckoned he was lucky when the old man agreed.

He was signing his name to the last letter with a heartfelt feeling of relief when the door was opened gently and Stukes came in with a silver tray. On it was a decanter of brandy and a siphon of soda water, together with two cut-glass tumblers.

He found a place on the writing-table and set the tray down carefully.

'Thank you, Stukes,' said Rayner, reaching for an envelope, and beginning to address it.

The butler waited hesitantly.

'Excuse me, sir. That tramp has come back.'

Rayner looked up sharply.

'Come back, has he? How do you know?'

'Thomas, the gardener saw him, sir. He'd lit a little fire on the fringe of Denham Wood and was cooking something over it.'

Rayner frowned. He helped himself to a

cigarette from the box in front of him and lit it.

'The same man, was it?' he asked.

'Thomas says so, sir,' replied Stukes. 'Very ragged sort of chap, dirty, with a stubbly beard and longish hair . . . '

'H'm! I told him to clear off when I found him camping out there last week. I don't like him being there. Never could stomach tramps. Don't get many round here as a rule.'

'No, sir.'

'I'll have a word with Inspector Trafford, I think. Where's my daughter?'

'Miss Rayner went out after dinner, sir. She hasn't come back yet.'

'All right, Stukes,' said Rayner. 'If you see her when she comes in tell her I'd like to see her, will you?'

The butler inclined his head and withdrew. Rayner stamped his letters and gathered them into a bundle ready to put in the postbag. Rising, he stretched himself, and poured out a stiff brandy and soda, carried it over to one of the easy chairs before the fire and sat down.

It was very pleasant, here, he thought

— peaceful and quiet after a strenuous life that had taken him half round the world. Cities held no attraction for him. He had had enough of noise and turmoil. There was too much rush and bustle in this present age.

Trencham Close was an old, rambling mansion standing in a fair acreage of wooded grounds on the borders of Hampshire, and, Rayner, looking round for a suitable place to live in on his return from abroad, had seen the place and instantly decided that it was just what he wanted.

Sir Percival Trench had been unmarried. There was no near relation to inherit the estate, only a distant cousin who was the next of kin and who was quite willing, even eager, to sell the old house and its contents for a very reasonable price. Sir Percival, who was generally supposed to be a rich man, had died practically penniless, so the cousin would have found it difficult to keep up the estate in any case.

Rayner, his wife had died abroad, moved in with his daughter, taking over those servants who were prepared to stay on, and settled down to enjoy the English countryside which they both loved. They considered themselves very lucky to have found such a lovely home, particularly as it was complete with an existing staff. Rayner was not a rich man but he was comfortably off, and he liked the life that a small village offered. His daughter, Marian had similar tastes and the moment they saw Trencham Close they decided it was the ideal place in which to settle down.

As the overseas sales director of a large firm of electronic engineers, his life had been spent travelling to various parts of the world and now that he had retired he was glad of the chance to relax in such a pleasant place as Bishop's Trencham which the march of progress had, for the time being, passed by.

He had just finished his brandy and soda and was gazing at the fire in lazy contentment when his daughter burst into the room.

She was of medium height and slim but with a slimness that had all the right curves in the right places. Her hair was neither gold nor red but a cunning blend of both and she wore it shoulder length.

'I thought you didn't know anyone down here?' she said breathlessly. 'Apart from the people who live in the village . . . '

He stared at her.

'Don't know what you mean, my dear,' he began, but she interrupted him.

'I was coming through Church Passage on the way home,' she said, 'when a man stopped me. 'Excuse me,' he said, 'are you Miss Rayner?' I said, 'Yes, I am,' and he gave me this note and asked me if I'd give it to you.'

She held out a square envelope.

'How extraordinary!' said Rayner, taking the letter and frowning at it. 'This man was a stranger?'

'Well, I've never seen him before,' she declared. 'He was a queer-looking chap. Very thin and pale — looked as if he'd just come out of hospital . . . '

Rayner looked at the superscription on the envelope. It was printed in rather straggly letters, with a ball-pointed pen apparently.

Putting his thumb under the flap he ripped the envelope open. Inside was a single sheet of paper. On it, also printed with a ball-pen, was a brief message:

Put the book on the sundial. If you keep what is not yours you must pay the penalty.

There was no signature.

'What does it mean?' asked the girl, who had been peering over his shoulder. 'What book?'

Her father shrugged his broad shoulders.

'I haven't the faintest idea,' he declared. 'Must have mistaken me for someone else. I know nothing about any book . . . '

His daughter pursed her lips.

'I scent a mystery!' she said. 'How lovely! That's all it wanted to make this whole place perfect.'

In the days that followed she was to get all the mystery she desired — and quite a lot that she would rather have done without!

2

Dick Farrell ran up the steps of the wide entrance to the offices of the *Daily*

Messenger, grinned at the porter, and made his way to the news editor's room.

Mr. Thimb looked up from his desk. He was a lanky, raw-boned man with a weary expression of eye and a complete lack of faith in the human race and the future of the world in general.

'There you are,' said Dick cheerily, putting some sheets of typing down on the desk. 'My last job for three weeks!'

'Why?' demanded Mr. Thimb.

'My holiday starts from noon,' said Dick. 'You know that very well. I shan't see your happy face for three whole weeks . . . '

'If this stuff you've brought me isn't better than the last, you won't see it again!' grunted the news editor. He picked up the thin sheets of copy paper and looked at them gloomily. 'So you're off on holiday, eh? What are you doing — fishing?'

'Well, I was, but I've had an invitation from a chap I know in the country — little village named Bishop's Trencham — to spend a few days with him. Might get some fishing later on.'

'I suppose you might as well loaf about the country as loaf about Fleet Street!' remarked Mr. Thimb. 'If you should come across anything worth printing don't forget to let us know, will you?'

He spoke sarcastically, never dreaming that at the peaceful village of Bishop's Trencham, Dick Farrell was to run into a story that made front page headlines for the *Messenger* and filled the soured life of its news editor with the nearest approach to joy that he knew.

Dick had met Charles Rayner just before the latter had bought Trencham Close. The meeting had taken place in the charge-room of a suburban police station! Dick had been gathering news of a gang responsible for a series of burglaries when Rayner had been brought in suffering from the shock of a car accident which had happened almost outside the police station.

Rayner hadn't been hurt but he was severely shaken, and after the particulars of the accident had been taken down, Dick had offered to accompany him to his hotel. Rayner had gratefully accepted. He had insisted that the reporter should come in for a drink and meet his daughter. From that time the friendship had ripened. Dick liked the big man who had a fund of stories to tell about his trips abroad, and he liked Marian. She had a sense of humour and was altogether a delightful companion. They went out together quite a lot while the Rayners were in London and he missed them when they had gone down to Bishop's Trencham to take up their residence in Trencham Close.

The invitation to spend a few days with them was unexpected and the letter containing it had puzzled Dick a little. It didn't actually mention in so many words that there was anything mysterious going on in the village, but it hinted at it, sufficiently to arouse Dick's curiosity.

After he left the offices of the *Daily Messenger*, Dick made his way home. He lived in a small flat in Bloomsbury, an old-fashioned place in one of the big houses that abound in that district, and which have been converted into flats and apartments, still retaining the fine old rooms, large and lofty, as in the bygone days when they had been private houses.

The first thing he did was to telephone to the friend with whom he had arranged to go on a fishing trip, but there was no reply. He was just putting down the receiver when there was a ring at the bell, and when he opened the door the man he had been trying to phone was standing on the step.

'I was just trying to phone you,' said Dick. 'Come in.'

Harry Glenn, a loose-limbed, rugged-faced man of about Dick's own age, followed him into the sitting-room.

'I hopped along to fix up the final details of this trip,' he said. 'What time do we leave . . . ?'

'We don't!' interrupted Dick. 'The trip's off!'

'Why? What's happened?'

Dick explained.

'I'm sorry to leave you in the cart, Harry,' he ended, 'but I fancy there's something funny going on . . . '

'How do you mean — funny?' demanded Glenn.

'Read the letter from Rayner. You'll see what I mean — at least I think you will.'

He tossed over the letter, and Harry Glenn scanned it quickly.

'H'm! Yes . . . ' He frowned. 'I seem to remember that Rayner's got a remarkably attractive daughter . . . '

'That's got nothing to do with it! Marian's a jolly good sort but she's not my type. I've got an instinct about these things and I believe I might run into something exciting.'

'I think I'll come to Bishop's Trencham too,' said Glenn. 'Any objection?'

'Well, I can't very well invite you to stay at Trencham Close,' began Dick, and the other broke in quickly.

'You don't have to,' he said. 'I suppose there's a village inn or something of the sort? I can put up there. I only met Marian Rayner once, but I wouldn't mind meeting her again . . . '

'I suppose there's nothing to stop you, if you want to come,' said Dick. 'It's a free country . . . '

'Don't sound so enthusiastic! I won't cramp your style with the lovely Marian . . . '

'I've told you, there's nothing like that!'

'All right then! When do we leave?'

'I'm catching a train in two hours time. You'll have to hurry . . . '

'I'm already packed for our trip that isn't!' said Glenn calmly. 'I'll go and collect my luggage and meet you at the station.'

'Fine! I've sent Rayner a wire to say what time I'm arriving. He said in his letter that he'd meet the train if I told him which one I was catching.'

'I wonder if he'll bring his daughter with him?' murmured Harry.

'I don't know. She must've made an impression on you. You only saw her for about five minutes, if I remember . . . '

'That was enough!' replied Glenn. 'Her image is indelibly printed on me 'eart!'

'Considering the number already there,' retorted Dick, 'your heart must be like a palimpsest!'

'I'm a big-hearted feller!' said Glenn. 'I'll be off! Don't be late at the station!'

2

1

Dusk had fallen, and with it a thin, damp, ground mist that struck a penetrating chill, when the train pulled up at the little station of Bishop's Trencham.

As Dick and Glenn got out on to the small wooden platform, a large, stout figure loomed through the fog and greeted them with a cheery 'Hello.'

'Jolly good of you to come,' said Rayner. He looked at Glenn, and Dick introduced him and explained.

'We were going on a fishing holiday together. Glenn thought he'd like to come down with me . . . '

'I won't trespass on your hospitality,' put in Harry. 'I can fix up at the village pub . . . '

'You'll do nothing of the kind,' said Rayner firmly. 'Only too happy to have you with us. The more the merrier, eh?'

15

He led the way down the platform, through the tiny booking-office, and out in to a cobbled yard. Here a car was waiting with its lights cutting a broad swathe through the mist.

With the doubtful assistance of an ancient porter, who mostly looked on, sucking his teeth, the luggage was stowed in the boot, and they got into the car.

'Shan't be long before we're home,' said Rayner. 'I expect you can do with a spot of something to drive out this infernal fog, eh?'

He shot out of the cobbled yard and turned into a narrow road. The fog was rapidly getting thicker but Rayner drove at a fairly fast speed. Presently, they came to a lane, so narrow that the hedges on either side brushed the car. Rather to Dick's uneasiness, Rayner increased his speed.

'There's no risk of running into anything here,' he explained, almost as though he could read Dick's thoughts. 'This lane is never used by anyone except me. It only leads to the house. Practically an extension of the drive.'

'Pretty lonely round here, isn't it?' said Glenn.

16

Rayner nodded.

'Nearest house is three miles away,' he replied. 'There's a small cottage on the hillside at the back. It was empty until a short while ago. Don't know who the people are who're living there now. Haven't seen 'em.'

At the end of the lane they swung through a gate between a pair of stone pillars, and as they rounded a bend the lights of the house appeared, shining blearily through the fog. Rayner brought the car to a stop in front of a short flight of worn stone steps.

The sound of the car must have been heard for as they got out the door opened and Stukes came down the steps.

'There'll be an extra guest, Stukes,' said Rayner, as he got out of the car. 'Mr. Glenn is staying with us. See that a room is prepared, will you?'

'Very good, sir,' said the butler.

'The luggage is in the boot,' said Rayner. 'Come and get warm.'

They followed him into a wide and spacious hall, the warmth of which was welcome after the damp cold outside. A log-fire blazed cheerfully in the big fireplace.

Rayner led the way over to a door on the right.

'Come and have a drink,' he said. 'Stukes will show you your rooms when he's attended to the luggage.'

The dining-room into which they followed their host was panelled in old oak which reflected the glow of the fire, a pleasant room, solid and comfortable, with a long refectory table down the centre, and an enormous sideboard occupying almost the whole of one side.

'What's it to be?' asked Rayner. 'Whisky?'

'Just what the doctor ordered,' said Glenn. 'It's very good of you, sir, to put me up . . .'

'Nonsense!' Rayner picked up a bottle of John Haig from an array of bottles on the sideboard. 'Only too pleased. Whisky for you, Farrell?'

'Please,' said Dick.

Rayner poured out three generous helpings of Haig.

'Soda or water?'

'Water for me,' said Dick. 'Soda spoils a good whisky.'

They both preferred water and by the time they had finished the drinks, Stukes was ready to show them to their rooms.

'Don't bother to dress,' said Rayner. 'We're very homely folk, and if you want anything just ask for it.'

The rooms that had been allotted to them were side by side at the end of a long corridor which apparently ran the entire length of the house.

'Pretty snug here, eh?' remarked Glenn. 'Nice of the old boy to put me up. I wonder where the attractive daughter is?'

'Heard you were coming and locked herself in her room, I expect,' grunted Dick. 'Hurry up and get washed, if you wash!' he added, and dodged the clothes brush that Harry hurled at him.

When they entered the drawing-room, later, Marian and her father were waiting for them. The girl was pleased to see them but Dick thought she looked a little strained. But she was certainly attractive.

The dinner gong sounded almost at once and they went into the dining-room. The meal was a pleasant one, simple but beautifully cooked and impeccably served by the old butler. With it they drank a vintage claret, a bin of which Rayner said he had taken over with the house.

Coffee was served in the drawing-room with a Hennessy brandy that added perfection to an excellent dinner. Dick, who had been waiting for an opportunity to bring the subject up, lit a cigarette and said:

'I rather gathered from your letter that certain things had been happening here that rather puzzled you.'

'That's putting it mildly,' said Marian. 'We seem to have unearthed a mystery — at least it's queer.'

'Tell me all about it,' said Dick.

'It started with the tramps,' answered Rayner.

'The tramps?'

The stout man nodded.

'Yes. They were camping in a little clearing on the fringe of Denham Wood. They were warned off but they came back . . . '

'We don't know that there was more than one,' put in the girl. 'Only one was seen at a time and . . . '

'I'm sure that there was more than

20

one,' broke in her father. 'Although, I'll admit, it wasn't easy to tell. They looked very much alike . . . '

'What did they do, or what did *he* do?' asked Dick

'Nothing!' said Rayner. 'Only made a fire and did some cooking. But they kept on coming back . . . '

'But that isn't all,' said Marian quickly. 'Tell them about the message — about the book . . . '

Rayner did so.

'I've got the letter, if you can call it that,' he ended. 'Put it in my pocket to show you.'

He took it out of his inside breast pocket and gave it to Dick. He read it and passed it on to Harry Glenn.

'You don't know anything about this book, I take it?' asked Dick.

Rayner shook his head.

'Nothing at all.'

'What was this man like who stopped you?'

'Thin and very pale,' answered Marian. 'He looked terribly ill . . . '

'But you'd never seen him before?'

'No, never.'

'How do you connect this man and the letter with the tramp or tramps?' asked Glenn.

'Well, we don't have any proof that they're connected,' said Rayner.

'But you think they are?'

'It seems possible — don't you think so?'

'What makes you think so?'

'The fact that they keep on coming back. It looks to me that the house is being watched . . . '

'For you to put this book on the sundial?' asked Harry Glenn.

'For something — I don't pretend to know what,' said Rayner.

'It's very exciting, isn't it?' said Marian. 'Just like a thriller story!'

Dick finished his brandy.

'Who did this house belong to before you bought it?' he asked abruptly.

'Sir Percival Trench, belonged to the family for years. Poor chap broke his neck while out hunting. No relatives except a cousin. I bought the place from him . . . '

'What did that include?'

'Everything!'

'The entire contents?'

'Yes. We hadn't any furniture of our own and this was just the sort of stuff we like. Can't stand this modern nonsense. Made out of old packing-cases most of it . . . '

'What do you know about Trench?'

Rayner shrugged his broad shoulders.

'Practically nothing!' he declared. 'Usual kind of country gentleman. Very well liked in the district. He'd recently got engaged to be married . . . '

'To be married?' echoed Glenn. 'How old was he, then?'

'Sixty-eight, I believe,' answered Rayner. 'She was comparatively young — only thirty-five. She lives at Abbey Lodge.'

'In the village?' asked Dick.

'About fifteen miles away,' said Marian. 'Wasn't there a will?'

'None was found,' said Rayner. 'The cousin got what there was. There was practically no money. That is why the cousin was so keen on accepting my offer to buy the place . . . '

'Perhaps there *is* a will, hidden in the book,' put in Glenn. 'That's why someone is so anxious to get hold of it . . . '

'Is there anything among the contents of the house that might be very valuable?' said Dick. 'You know the sort of thing I mean — a picture or china, anything of that sort?'

'There might be,' said Rayner rather dubiously. 'If there is I know nothing about it . . . '

'It's only an idea . . . '

'The chap who gave you that letter might be a bit mental, Miss Rayner,' said Glenn. 'You say he looked as if he'd been ill . . . '

'He did,' said the girl. 'And please don't call me 'Miss Rayner,' call me 'Marian.''

'So far as I can see,' said Dick, 'there's not very much anyone can do. If you ignore this letter and don't put the book, whatever-it-is, on the sundial, either something will happen or nothing will happen . . . '

'Profound deduction by our tame investigator!' murmured Glenn. 'Really remarkable!'

'You know what I mean, idiot!' retorted Dick. 'We must just wait and see. The next episode, if any, may supply us with a clue to the whole thing.'

2

Dick Farrell stood at the window of his bedroom looking out at the view. The white mist had vanished, and the countryside was dimly visible in the light of a sliver of moon. He hadn't begun to undress when Harry Glenn came in.

'I think I'm going to enjoy this better than our original idea of a fishing holiday,' he remarked, sitting down on the side of the bed. 'I don't think I've ever met such an attractive girl.'

'You make it fairly obvious!' grunted Dick. 'Every time you look at her you remind me of a sick cow!'

'You've no sense of beauty! Have you seen the graceful way she walks across a room? And the way she smiles? That cute little dimple . . . '

'Oh cut it out!' snapped his friend. 'Come over here!'

Glenn got up and joined him at the window.

'What is it?' he asked.

'What do you make of that?' Farrell pointed into the semi-darkness.

At the end of the wide lawn was a row of poplars, dark and sinister, like funeral plumes, and beyond them the hillside rose up to its wooded crest. Somewhere, near the top, a tiny speck of light winked redly.

'What is it?' asked Glenn.

Dick shook his head.

'I don't know. I've been watching it for some time.'

The little star of crimson light continued to shine brightly for some seconds, and then abruptly it went out.

'Must be a light from some window,' said Glenn.

'Too small. Looked more like a torch to me . . .'

'What would anyone be doing with a torch out there? It was red, too . . .'

'Could be some sort of signal,' said Dick. 'It must be pretty near that cottage old Rayner was telling us about.'

'There's no other house within three miles so I suppose it would be. But who are they signalling to?'

'Search me! One of the tramps perhaps . . .'

'What for?'

'Your guess is as good as mine.'

They continued to watch for several minutes but the light did not appear again. Dick was in the act of turning away from the window, when Glenn suddenly gripped his arm, went over to the switch and plunged the room in darkness.

'What the devil do you think you're doing?' began Farrell, but his friend stopped him with a violent push.

'Shut up!' he said. 'I thought I saw something move in the shadow of the house. Yes! Look! I knew I was right!'

Dick peered in the direction Glenn was pointing. A muffled figure came cautiously from the shadow of a clump of bushes and began to hurry across the lawn. Midway it paused and looked back towards the house.

Dick gave a gasp as he saw the face in the moonlight.

It was Marian Rayner!

3

1

They looked at each other and it was Glenn who was the first to speak.

'There's no reason why she shouldn't take a stroll, is there?' he asked unconvincingly. 'Perhaps she wanted to get some air . . . '

'Rather a strange thing to do — at this time of night.'

'Oh, I don't know . . . ' Glenn looked out of the window again. The girl had disappeared in the shadow at the end of the lawn.

'I wonder if that's what the light was for?' muttered Dick. 'It was obviously a signal to someone.'

'This is going to make things a bit awkward,' said Glenn. He took out a packet of cigarettes, took one, and held it out to his friend.

'I see what you mean.' Dick took a

cigarette. Glenn snapped on a lighter and lit both. 'It may not have anything to do with this other business . . . '

'We don't know what this other business is, do we?' Glenn blew out a cloud of smoke. 'I can't imagine Marian being mixed up in anything shady. I'm sure she doesn't know anything more than we do. It could be a — a boy friend, couldn't it?'

'Well, we can't very well spy on our hostess,' said Dick. He pulled the curtains over the window and switched the light on again. 'I think the best we can do is go to bed! How do you feel like getting up early and inspecting the countryside?'

'Why? What's on your mind?'

'I'd like to have a look at that cottage,' said Dick.

'All right — I'm game.'

'I'll call you early.' He took his friend gently by the arm and piloted him to the door. 'Sleep well!'

It seemed to Harry Glenn that he had scarcely closed his eyes before he was awakened by a hand shaking him vigorously. He opened his eyes and blinked up at Dick resentfully.

'What's the time?' he demanded.

'Just after five!' answered his friend. 'Come on, get up!'

'Oh, I say, look here . . . '

'Get up!'

Glenn sat up in bed.

'It's jolly cold,' he grumbled.

'Hurry up and get dressed then . . . '

'I can't see any reason why we've got to be so early,' grunted Harry. 'Five! It's dark!'

'I'll give you five minutes,' said Dick. 'Hurry!'

With a sigh of resignation, Harry Glenn got out of bed and dressed quickly.

Charles Rayner's household had not yet stirred. The entire house was silent as they made their way stealthily down the wide staircase and let themselves out by a side door.

The early morning air smelt cold and sweet as they hurried across the lawn. There was a heavy dew and a thin white mist hung in the air. There was no sign yet of the dawn. The crescent moon had gone, but the sky was full of stars. The white mist was only a ground mist, barely reaching up to their heads, and hanging in long swathes, floating like filmy scarves.

Crossing the lawn they came to a wooden fence that ran along the line of the poplars.

'There must be a gate or something,' said Dick, pausing and looking about him. 'Let's try this way.'

He turned to the left and walked along the fence until presently, he came to a gate set in the wooden fence. The gate was locked with a padlock but it was only a low affair and they easily climbed over it. Beyond was a narrow lane that appeared to run parallel with the fence. It was evidently little used for the surface was unscarred by any wheel-track. On the opposite side of the lane was a thin, straggling hedge and beyond that again the hillside of coarse grassland rose gently up to the wooded crest.

'Come on,' said Dick. 'This way.'

They found a break in the hedge and scrambled through. The hillside was covered with patchy gorse and two or three small groups of trees. Dick pointed to the ground by the break in the hedge.

'Looks as if this way was used pretty frequently,' he said.

'Are you thinking of Marian?' asked Harry.

'Not particularly. It's probably a short cut to somewhere.'

'Used by the immense crowds round here?' remarked Glenn sarcastically.

'Yes, I see what you mean,' said Dick. 'Well, let's press on!'

They made their way up the slope. It was easy going at first but after a while the slope got steeper and steeper.

'I must say,' panted Harry, 'that this is hardly my idea of a pleasant holiday . . . '

'You're out of condition!' grunted Dick.

'What about you? You're puffing and blowing like a grampus!'

'Save your breath . . . Good God! Look there!'

Dick stopped dead and pointed to a clump of trees. Glenn stopped too and uttered a gasp.

From the branch of one of the trees, swaying in the slight breeze, hung the body of a man!

For a moment they stood staring silently at the unpleasant object. It was Harry who made the first move.

'Who can it be?' he muttered, and moved forward, but Dick restrained him.

'Be careful,' he warned. 'I don't think we'd better touch anything. It's a job for the police. We don't want to go and mess up any traces . . . '

'He may be still alive . . . '

'Yes, I suppose we'd better make sure.'

He picked his way carefully towards the tree and looked up at the hanging figure. The feet were almost on a level with his shoulder. He could see the face now, congested and distorted, and there was little doubt that the man was dead. He was short and rather stout. He was without an overcoat and his worn suit was of some brown material.

'He's dead right enough,' said Dick, putting his hand on the rigid limbs. 'Been dead for a long time, too. Looks like murder . . . '

'Murder!' broke in the horrified Glenn.

'How do you know he was murdered?'

'Somebody has climbed that tree wearing nailed boots,' said Dick. 'Look, you can see the marks . . . '

'It might have been him . . . ?'

'He's wearing rubber-soled shoes. We'd better get in touch with the police. Perhaps they'll know who this poor chap is. I'll stay here if you'll go back to the house and phone.'

Harry nodded.

'Wake Rayner and tell him what's happened, but don't say anything to anyone else.'

Glenn nodded again and hurried off down the steep incline. Left alone Dick lit a cigarette, moving away from the tree and its unpleasant burden. He had never expected his morning excursion to end in this gruesome fashion. Maybe there was more in Charles Rayner's little puzzle than he had at first supposed.

The slope of the hillside continued on past the clump of trees from one of which the dead man hung, and he looked to see if there was any sign of the cottage Rayner had mentioned. But the fringe of the woodland hid it, if it was there.

He turned and looked in the direction of Trencham Close. The dawn was breaking and he could make out the window of his bedroom without much difficulty. The spot where he was standing must be very near the place from which the red light had flickered. Perhaps that star-point, shining through the night, had brought this unknown man to his death?

It was getting light quite quickly but it was also cold. To keep himself warm Dick started to walk up and down. A splash of colour on a stunted gorse bush attracted his attention and he went to see what it was.

It was a little crumpled ball of flimsy silk. The moment he picked it up he saw that it was a woman's scarf! The type of thing that a girl would wrap round her neck on a cold night . . .

A waft of perfume, faint but unmistakable, reached his nostrils. Marian Rayner's!

The girl must have been here last night! It was where she was going when they had seen her leave the house. Dick felt distinctly uneasy. Surely she couldn't be mixed up with the murder? It seemed impossible. Probably there was a simple explanation. In the meanwhile it would be better if the police did not know about the scarf. He folded it carefully and put it in his pocket.

There was a stone near the gorse bush and Dick sat down, threw away the stub of his cigarette and lit another.

Could the girl have got herself into any kind of trouble? Blackmail, perhaps? But that would hardly account for the strange man who had given her the letter for Rayner. Or the persistence of the tramps in the vicinity . . .

He was still speculating when Glenn returned with Rayner. The big man looked troubled, with worried lines round his eyes.

'This is a dreadful business,' he said, panting from the exertion of the climb. 'Terrible! I've telephoned the police and they're coming at once.'

'Do you know the man?' asked Dick.

Rayner reluctantly walked over to the tree and looked up.

'No, he's a stranger to me,' he declared.

'I don't know many people round here, you know. Could be somebody from the village. Perhaps Inspector Trafford will know him.'

'What sort of man is Trafford?'

Rayner shrugged his broad shoulders.

'Not very intelligent, I'm afraid. I haven't had much experience of rural policemen but I should say he was a typical specimen . . . '

'The best thing he can do is to call in Scotland Yard,' said Dick.

'I doubt if he'll want to do that,' answered Rayner. 'He'll want to carry it through on his own. He's got quite a good opinion of himself.'

'It'll depend on the chief constable, anyway,' said Dick. 'Where's this cottage you were talking about?'

'It's up there.' Rayner pointed to the wood. 'Just through the first fringe of trees.'

'Do you think that this chap's got anything to do with it? You said that the place had recently been taken . . . '

'About three weeks ago,' said Rayner.

'Let's go and see,' said Dick, getting

up. 'You wait here, Harry, for the police. Rayner and I will go up to the cottage and see what we can find.'

Leaving Glenn they set off up the rest of the slope and entered the fringe of the wood. There was a small clearing amid the thickly growing trees in the centre of which stood a thatched cottage. It was surrounded by a tiny garden which was overgrown with weeds.

The place was in pretty bad repair and there was no sign of life, but Dick and Rayner went up to the blistered front door and knocked.

They waited but there was no reply. Dick was in the act of knocking again when he heard the sound of movement within. There was the rattle of a chain, followed by the rasp of rusty bolts. The door was opened and Dick got one of the greatest shocks he had ever had in his life.

'Dick Farrell!' exclaimed the man in the dressing-gown who had opened the door. 'What on earth are you doing here?'

'Felix Heron!' ejaculated Dick. 'I might ask you the same question!'

4

1

Felix Heron was the first to recover from the surprise of this unexpected meeting.

'Come in,' he invited. 'You're Charles Rayner, aren't you?'

The astonished Rayner nodded.

'Just wait in here while I go and wake my wife,' said Heron. He led the way into a small sitting-room, shabbily furnished but with two fairly comfortable easy chairs. 'Sit down, I won't be a minute.'

He went out and Rayner turned to Dick.

'Who is he?' he asked in a low voice.

'It's not very easy to tell you,' answered Farrell. 'He's not an ordinary private detective, or a special agent, nor is he a solicitor, but he combines all three, if you understand me.'

Clearly Rayner did not.

'You mean he works for the police?' he asked.

'Sometimes, sometimes he works for the Government. He's a kind of specialist. In anything out of the ordinary Felix Heron is consulted. I've met him several times . . . '

'What's he doing here?'

'I've no idea. He was the last person I expected to see.'

Rayner grunted.

'This place seems to have become the focal point for all sorts of queer things,' he muttered.

Heron came back carrying a tray from which came the pleasant aroma of freshly made coffee. He poured out three cups and gave two to his unexpected visitors.

'Thelma will be down in a minute,' he said. 'I've taken her up a cup of coffee. Now, what's the idea of this early call?'

Dick explained briefly.

'I know nothing of the murder,' said Heron. 'I can tell you about the light you saw. I was the culprit. I was signalling to Thelma.' He took a sip of coffee. 'I'm very interested in these tramps — there are two of them and they take it in turns to camp out near Denham Wood. For the moment they've gone but I expect they'll come back . . . '

'May I ask,' put in Rayner, 'what you are doing here?'

Heron considered for a moment before he replied.

'I shall have to ask you to treat what I tell you in confidence, both of you.' They promised and he went on: 'Do you know a lady named Dorothy Lessinger?'

'She was the woman who was engaged to poor Trench,' said Rayner in surprise.

'You know her?'

Rayner shook his head.

'I've only heard of her . . . '

'Well, it's at her request that we're here,' said Heron. 'She's under the impression that Trench's death was not the result of an accident!'

It was a morning of shocks. Rayner gaped at Felix in open-mouthed amazement.

'You can't be serious!' he exclaimed.

'I am — quite serious,' said Heron.

'But — but . . . he was killed in the hunting field,' stammered Charles Rayner.

41

'His horse threw him and he broke his neck . . . '

'That is the general belief. But Miss Lessinger is doubtful. She has told no one of her suspicions except me. I must say that I share her doubt!'

Rayner took out a handkerchief and wiped his face.

'I'm completely staggered!' he declared. 'I never imagined that . . . '

'Naturally,' said Heron. 'The coroner was perfectly satisfied and so was everyone else — except Miss Lessinger.'

'Why was she suspicious?' asked Dick.

'That's rather a long story,' said Heron. 'I'll have to postpone it until later. I want to have a look at this man before Inspector Trafford gets on the scene . . . '

'Do you know Trafford?' asked Rayner.

'Only by sight.' He looked round as Thelma Heron came in. She wasn't tall but she gave the appearance of litheness. She was wearing a housecoat over pyjamas and her dark hair fell about her shoulders. She looked at them from very deep blue eyes and smiled at Dick.

'Hello,' she said. 'I didn't expect to see

you this morning.'

'The surprise is mutual, Mrs. Heron,' said Dick.

Heron introduced Rayner.

'We're going out, dear,' he said. 'There's been a murder . . . '

'A murder!' she echoed. 'Where?'

He explained.

'Come and join us when you're dressed,' he said.

She agreed, and they left the cottage and made their way quickly to the place where the dead man swung gently from the branch of the tree.

Harry Glenn was pacing up and down but there was no sign of the police. He looked surprised when he saw Felix Heron and even more surprised when Dick introduced them.

The sun was up, pale and without heat as yet, and Heron went straight over to the body. He looked up at the liver-coloured face and Rayner saw his expression change slightly. But Heron said nothing.

'He's been dead for several hours, I should think,' he remarked. 'Show me these nail marks you told me about.'

Dick pointed them out and Heron nodded.

'Yes, it looks as though the murderer climbed the tree and lay in wait. Probably dropped the noose over his victim's neck and jerked it tight, jumped down with the rope still in his hand, hauled this poor chap up and tied the end round the trunk.'

'I thought it was something of the sort,' said Dick. 'Which means that he'd arranged a meeting under this tree?'

'That's about it,' Heron stopped, and looked round as there came the faint sound of voices. Coming up the incline were three men. The foremost was a large, round-faced man in the uniform of a police inspector. He was followed by a constable. Bringing up the rear, and obviously out of breath, was a tall, thinnish man, who, judging from the fact that he was carrying a small black bag, they concluded was a doctor.

Inspector Trafford came up to them, panting and puffing. He eyed them ungraciously through small, rather pig-like eyes.

44

'What's all this, eh?' he demanded. 'I got your message, Mr. Rayner. Somethin' about a murder, eh? There seems to be enough of you here, eh?'

'It's a dreadful affair,' answered Rayner. 'Mr. Farrell and Mr. Glenn, who are staying with me, made the discovery . . . '

'I'll take their statements later,' interrupted the inspector. He went over and stared at the body, screwing up his mouth in a small 'O.' 'H'm,' he commented. 'Why did you jump to the conclusion that it was murder, eh? This man may have hanged himself, eh?'

'There are signs of another person having climbed the tree,' explained Dick.

Inspector Trafford looked at the marks and frowned.

'It's too early yet for me to form any conclusions,' he remarked portentously. 'Better cut this poor feller down at once, eh?'

'I'll climb up and cut the rope while you and the constable take the weight,' suggested Felix Heron.

'No need for that. We can untie the knot . . . '

'It would be better if you didn't. The knot might prove to be of importance.'

This had not occurred to Trafford and he was a little disgruntled. He stared at Heron in no very friendly way.

'And who are you?' he demanded.

'My name is Heron,' answered Felix. 'I've just moved into the cottage up there.' He nodded in the direction of the wood.

'Oh, I see.' The inspector regarded him suspiciously. 'You've just moved in, eh?'

'Exactly!' Thelma Heron in slacks and a pullover was coming down the hillside towards them. 'This is my wife.'

'I shall want to talk to you both presently,' said Trafford. He called the constable and between them they got the body down.

'Now, doctor, perhaps you'll have a look at him,' said the inspector, wiping his face after his exertions.

The thin man came forward. Kneeling beside the dead man he made a quick examination.

'He died from dislocation of the neck and suffocation,' he said. 'That's all I can tell you until after the P.M. He's been dead, roughly, about five hours.'

'That would be the result of hanging, eh?' asked Trafford.

'Yes.'

'Thank you, doctor.' Trafford took the thin man's place and with clumsy fingers began to search the pockets. There was not much among the collection. A cheap watch, a handful of silver and a few coppers, a propelling pencil, and a crushed packet containing three cigarettes. That was all. There was no sign of a wallet. If the man had carried one it had been taken by his killer.

The inspector rose to his feet with an expression of disappointment.

'Not much there, eh? I was hoping that there'd be some means of identification . . .'

'I can identify him,' remarked Felix Heron quietly.

His totally unexpected words had the effect of surprising everybody, including the inspector.

'You know this man, eh?' he asked.

'I *knew* him, yes. His name is Mellins,

George Mellins. For some years he has been a police informer . . . '

'A police informer, eh? How do you know all this, eh?'

'I came across him in the course of my business,' said Heron.

Inspector Trafford stared at him, his little eyes were full of suspicion.

'I think you'd better explain a bit more clearly, eh? It strikes me that you know a lot more than you've told me . . . '

'I know nothing at all,' said Heron. 'I should very much like to know what Mellins was doing in this district . . . '

'And I should like to know what *you're* doing here,' said the inspector. 'What is this business you were talking about just now, eh?'

'I'm a specialist,' replied Heron with a twinkle in his eye. 'A specialist in all sorts of things. If you're at all doubtful about me I suggest that you ring up the Foreign Office. They'll put your fears at rest.'

'The Foreign Office?'

'You could also try the Prime Minister. I'm sure he'd be only too pleased to vouch for my integrity . . . '

'Are you trying to pull my leg?' demanded Trafford, his large face deepening in colour.

'Certainly not!'

'You wouldn't like me to try the Queen, eh?'

'Her Majesty would be delighted to give me an excellent reference!' said Heron blandly. 'You're wasting your time on me, inspector. Better get on with the job and leave me out of it!'

Heron turned away leaving Trafford purple in the face and on the verge of an explosion. He mastered his temper with an effort and devoted his attention to Dick and Harry Glenn. He insisted on a detailed account of how they had come to make the discovery and noted what they told him in a large pocket-book.

'I shall want to see all of you later,' he said. 'I mean *all* of you!' He glared at Heron, and Thelma gave him a sweet smile. 'I'm going to the station now. You stay here, Harrison, an' I'll send up a stretcher for the body.'

The constable nodded, and gathering up the contents of the dead man's pockets in a handkerchief, Inspector Trafford marched off with the doctor.

Dick chuckled.

'You certainly dealt with that nit-wit,' he said. 'He'll probably ring up the lot!'

'I don't mind if he does,' said Heron.

Charles Rayner smiled.

'Suppose you and your wife come back with us to the house?' he suggested. 'I'd like to hear more about this business of Trench's death . . . '

2

It was still early and breakfast was waiting when they got back to Trencham Close. They were met in the hall by Stukes who looked worried and anxious.

'I'm glad you've returned, sir,' he said. 'It's about Miss Marian . . . '

'What about her?' demanded Rayner sharply.

'She's not in her room, sir.'

Dick exchanged a quick glance with Glenn.

'Perhaps she's gone out . . . '

'I don't think so, sir,' Stukes was apologetic at the contradiction. 'From what Alice says Miss Marian hasn't been to bed all night, sir.'

Dick remembered the scarf that was in his pocket, and the glimpse of the girl they had caught stealthily crossing the lawn.

'Not been to bed all night?' echoed Rayner. 'But that's ridiculous . . . '

'Perhaps you'd like to see Alice, sir?'

'Yes — send her to us at once,' ordered Rayner.

The butler hurried away and in a few seconds a young and rather pretty village girl in a maid's uniform appeared and looked at them nervously.

'What's this about Miss Marian?' asked Rayner.

'The bed 'adn't been slep' in, sir,' said Alice. 'When I took up the mornin' tea, the coverlet was still turned down, like what I'd left it last night.'

Rayner frowned.

'What can have happened to her?' he muttered.

'I don't know, sir.'

'Go and send Thomas to me,' said Rayner, and the girl hurried away. 'She must've gone out somewhere.'

Harry Glenn stirred uneasily and Dick gave him a warning glance. There was little doubt in his mind that Marian had not returned from her midnight excursion, but he did not intend to say anything yet. The girl might have some good reason for her absence, although it was certainly peculiar . . .

The gardener, Thomas, a healthy-looking man in his early forties, came in.

'You wanted me, sir?' he inquired respectfully.

'You've been working in the garden this morning?' asked Rayner. 'Have you seen anything of Miss Marian?'

Thomas shook his head.

'No, sir.'

'Were you working near the house?'

'I was clearin' that bed under the drawin'-room winders, sir.'

'I see. Thank you, Thomas.'

The gardener, looking a little puzzled, went away.

'I can't understand it at all,' declared

Rayner. He looked worried. 'She's never done anything like this before.'

'Has she any friends in the village?' asked Thelma.

'Not that I know. We haven't been here long enough. Marian's met the vicar, of course, and I believe she knows the woman at the post-office . . . '

'Nobody with whom she could have stayed the night?'

Rayner shook his head.

'No. Besides why should she?'

Nobody could answer this. They went up and looked at the girl's bedroom. It was quite obvious that the bed had never been slept in. A search of her wardrobe revealed that the dress she had been wearing the previous night together with a tweed coat were missing. So were a pair of brogues.

Dick, who had followed the search with growing uneasiness, pulled Harry on one side as they went back downstairs.

'Look here,' he whispered. 'We'll have to tell Rayner what we saw last night.'

'I suppose so,' said Harry, dubiously.

Dick told them what they had seen

from the bedroom window.

'I think she was wearing that coat,' he ended. 'She had a scarf round her head . . . '

Heron looked grave. 'I think we'd better start a search for her,' he said.

'You think something can have happened to her?' asked Rayner quickly. 'Something to do with this other business?'

'She might have had an accident. She could've twisted her ankle perhaps . . . '

A search-party was hastily organised and they searched the grounds and part of the surrounding country but there was no sign of the missing girl.

'I think I'd better get on to the police,' said the greatly worried Rayner. 'This looks serious . . . '

'I should,' agreed Heron. 'Unless for some reason your daughter's staying away of her own accord it could be very serious.'

As soon as they returned to the house Rayner went off to phone. While he was absent, Dick told Heron about the scarf.

'I didn't say anything to the police,' he

said, 'for obvious reasons. I haven't said anything to Rayner, either. She must have been close to the place where that fellow was killed . . . '

'It's not conclusive, is it?' said Thelma. 'Because her scarf was there doesn't prove that she was. Somebody could have taken it there.'

'If she saw something that she wasn't intended to see,' said Heron, and stopped but the expression of his face told them what he was thinking.

'But what was she doing up there on the hillside?' asked Dick.

'And where is she now?' put in Glenn. 'That's more important.'

'There's a big end to all this business,' said Felix Heron. 'The reason Miss Lessinger came to me was that Trench, several times before his fatal accident, hinted to her that he was afraid something might happen to him . . . '

'Why?'

Heron shook his head.

'He didn't tell her. But she says that for the last six weeks before he died he was a very frightened man . . . '

Charles Rayner came back from telephoning, in a furious temper.

'That man, Trafford, is a fool!' he declared angrily. 'No intelligence at all! I shall complain to his superiors . . . '

'What's he done?' asked Dick.

'He refuses to believe that anything could have happened to Marian,' growled Rayner. 'Says she must have gone off somewhere of her own accord. Hints that there's some man at the bottom of it! I gave him a piece of my mind, I can tell you!' He took out his handkerchief and mopped at his big face. 'I could do with a drink! Come into the dining-room!'

They followed him into the dining-room. The breakfast things had been cleared. They had had no time for the meal and it was now getting near lunch time.

'I'm going to have a large brandy,' said Rayner. 'What about the rest of you?'

'I'd like a sherry,' said Thelma.

'I've got some Dry Fly,' said Rayner.

'That's my favourite sherry,' said Thelma.

The others elected to have whisky and

Rayner produced some bottles from a cupboard in the huge sideboard. He poured. Thelma her Dry Fly, gave the other three large whiskies, and finally poured himself an extra large Hennessy. He gulped half of it quickly.

'That's better! I needed that!'

Dick was helping himself to water from a jug on the sideboard when Stukes came in hurriedly. The old man was excited and breathless.

'Excuse me, sir, but the gardener has just found this, sir. Pinned to the oak tree,' he said, holding out a dirty piece of paper.

Rayner snatched it from him.

'Look at this!' he exclaimed and thrust the paper at Heron. 'Look! What can we do?'

The message, in capitals, was brief and to the point:

PUT THE BOOK ON THE SUNDIAL TONIGHT IF YOU WISH TO SEE YOUR DAUGHTER ALIVE.

5

1

Felix Heron read the message twice with knitted brows. Instead of making any comment he looked over at the butler.

'This was pinned to an oak tree, you say?' he said.

'Yes, sir.'

'Where is this tree?'

'On the edge of the lawn, sir.'

'What can we do?' exclaimed Rayner. 'Marian's in danger . . . '

Felix Heron made a gesture to him to keep silent.

'I'd like a word with the gardener,' he said.

'Fetch him, will you,' ordered Rayner to the butler, and the old man bowed and went out. 'This is dreadful! Marian must have fallen into the hands of these people, whoever they are . . . '

'I don't think you have any immediate

cause for anxiety,' said Heron. He finished his whisky, picked up the bottle of John Haig and helped himself to another. 'They are using your daughter as a bargaining proposition. They want to frighten you into handing over the book. Once they kill her their advantage is gone.'

'Felix is right, Mr. Rayner,' said Thelma.

'They may do her some harm,' said Rayner, by no means reassured by this quite sensible argument.

'I doubt if she'll be hurt at all,' said Heron. 'The whole object is one of exchange — your daughter for this book. There would be no point at all in injuring her.'

'What the devil can this infernal book be!' said Rayner.

'That is what the whole affair is about,' Heron answered. 'I had no knowledge of this book until this morning but I should guess that it was this book, or the possession of it, that made Sir Percival Trench so scared . . . '

There was a tap at the door and the

gardener entered.

'Come in, Thomas,' said Heron. 'You found this paper on the oak tree, didn't you?'

'Yes, sir. I was goin' back from 'avin' a cup o' tea in the kitchen, when I saw it.'

'Is this oak tree visible from the kitchen?'

'Yes, sir.'

'But none of the servants saw anyone pin this up?'

'Not as I know, sir.'

'Did you ask them?'

'Well, no, sir. But they'd 'ave told me if they 'ad.'

'Well, thank you, Thomas,' said Heron and Rayner told the man he could go.

'What can we do next?' he asked a little helplessly. 'This has given me a dreadful shock! I wish to God we'd never come here!'

'Don't worry too much,' said Heron sympathetically. 'There's nothing much we *can* do at the moment. We might take a line of action later . . . '

'Pretend to carry out the demand?' asked Thelma.

Heron nodded.

'Always dead on the mark, aren't you, dear?' he said. 'Yes, we might do that. Although there's an element of danger. These people might get angry . . . '

'You mean,' said Dick, 'that we should put some book, any book, on the sundial?'

Heron nodded, but Harry Glenn looked dubious.

'Surely the people who sent that message will be on the lookout for something of the sort,' he said. 'It's such an obvious trap. Particularly after the discovery of Mellins's body . . . '

'We don't know that Mellins's death has anything to do with this book business . . . '

'You don't really believe that, do you?' put in Dick, and Heron smiled.

'Candidly, I don't,' he answered. 'The person who sent this message must be under the impression that Mr. Rayner knows all about this book. Otherwise, he would have given more details. Why should he think that?'

'Look,' said Dick, 'suppose you tell us

what you know. Why did this Miss Lessinger think that Trench's death wasn't an accident?'

'All right,' said Heron. 'You'd better sit down, it's quite a long story.'

They settled themselves in the easy chairs before the big fireplace, Thelma perching herself on the arm of her husband's chair, and Dick pulling out one of the dining chairs and straddling it.

'Well, in spite of the doctor's evidence and the fact that the coroner was satisfied,' said Heron, 'Miss Lessinger was convinced that there was something fishy about Trench's death. She had practically nothing to go on, except that for some time before the accident Trench appeared to be afraid of something happening to him. He wouldn't tell her what it was but he was definitely scared.'

He took a sip of his whisky and went on:

'I don't know whether you know the details of the accident, but briefly they were these: Trench got separated from the main hunt, and when they returned he was missing. A search party was sent to find him, and eventually he was discovered, stone-dead, lying a few yards from a high hedge that bordered a ploughed field. The doctor testified that he had died from a broken neck. The horse he had been riding was grazing quietly in a nearby meadow. It seemed obvious that Trench's death was an accident.

'When Miss Lessinger came to me, I was frankly sceptical. There seemed no ground to suspect foul play. However, she was so persistent that Thelma suggested that I might look into the matter . . . '

'She had an intuition that there was something wrong,' said Thelma. 'A very strong intuition. I don't think people should discount intuition.'

'There was something more practical,' said Heron. 'On the day after his death he had arranged to make a will leaving this house and everything he died possessed of to Miss Lessinger . . . '

'That wouldn't have done her much good,' grunted Rayner. 'The house is worth something but there wasn't much money, you know . . . '

Heron looked at him queerly.

'It will surprise you to learn that a year before he died, Sir Percival Trench was worth over two hundred thousand pounds,' he said.

It certainly did!

'Over two hundred thousand pounds!' echoed Rayner, his eyes almost popping from his head. 'Good God! What happened to it?'

'I'm coming to that,' said Heron. He finished his John Haig, and Thelma took his glass and put it on the table. 'The first thing I did was to go and see Trench's solicitors. Mr. Sedman was extremely helpful. He pooh-poohed the idea that there had been any funny business about his client's death, but he admitted that there *was* something extremely peculiar in the state of his affairs.'

He had them all interested now.

'For the last eighteen months Sir Percival Trench had been steadily selling all his securities. He had acquired in this manner two hundred and twenty thousand pounds. And nobody knows what has happened to that money!'

'His unfortunate cousin would like to

know,' said Rayner. He went over and poured himself another Hennessy. 'Anybody else like a drink?'

'I'd like another Dry Fly, please,' said Thelma. 'Go on, Felix, tell them the rest of it.' She took her glass over to Rayner and he refilled it.

'Sedman didn't know,' continued Heron. 'He asked once and was told to mind his own business. That money has vanished completely. What Trench did with it is a mystery. The cheques he received for the sale of his shares and other securities, he paid into his bank and immediately drew out the money in cash.'

'Two hundred and twenty thousand pounds is a whole lot of money,' said Harry Glenn.

Heron nodded.

'Exactly. It was the disappearance of this money that made me think there might be something in Miss Lessinger's suspicions after all. What could he have done with this huge sum? He hadn't re-invested it, at least so far as we could discover, and he hadn't bought anything . . .'

'Blackmail?' suggested Dick.

'That's what seems likely,' agreed Heron. 'But why should the blackmailer have killed him? Of course, if he *did* die as the result of an accident, that objection is overruled.'

'How does the book come into it?' asked Glenn.

'I couldn't say. I told you earlier that I knew nothing about it. I did know about the tramps, however. Miss Lessinger had heard about them camping out in Denham Wood. So I decided to come down here and see what I could pick up. After all, it was here that Trench had met his death. I didn't want to appear openly so I took the empty cottage. Thelma and I have taken it in turns to look out for the tramps, and I saw one of them once, but he was off before I could get near enough to see what he was like under the dirt. One thing, though. I'm pretty sure that he wasn't the genuine article. Tramps do not as a rule eat chicken breasts in aspic, particularly from Fortnum and Mason's, and that's what he'd had. I found the empty jar.'

He stopped and looked up as Stukes came in.

'Excuse me, sir,' said the butler, 'but there's a young lady called to see Miss Marian . . . '

'Who is she?' demanded Rayner in surprise. 'What's her name?'

'Mrs. Leyton, sir.'

Rayner uttered an exclamation of annoyance.

'Tell her that Miss Marian isn't at home,' he said curtly.

'I did, sir, but she said it was most important and could she wait.'

'Go back and tell Mrs. Leyton that we have no idea when Miss Marian will be back and therefore it's useless her waiting,' snapped Rayner.

'Just a minute,' interposed Felix Heron. 'Who is this woman?'

'She's an old school friend of Marian's,' said Rayner. 'They used to write to each other while we were abroad. Marian saw quite a lot of her when we got back. She's not the type of woman I approve . . . '

'I think we ought to see her, all the same,' said Heron.

'Why?'

'Does she live in London?'

'Yes. What has that got to do with it?'

'Has she been down here before to see your daughter?'

'No. I refused to let Marian invite her.'

'She wanted to?'

'Yes.'

'Don't you think it would be interesting to learn what has brought her down today?'

Rayner frowned. His heavy face was clouded but he nodded.

'All right,' he said grudgingly. 'Ask Mrs. Leyton to come in, Stukes.'

2

The girl whom the butler showed in a few seconds later was tall and decidedly pretty, in spite of the lines about her mouth and the bruise that disfigured her forehead.

She was dressed in an olive green raincoat, with a small hat to match, and she stood hesitantly just inside the doorway, her large, dark eyes surveying the group nervously.

She was quite young, she couldn't have been more than twenty-four or twenty-five, and she looked worried and exhausted.

'I — I'm very sorry to disturb you, Mr. Rayner,' she apologised, and her voice was soft and slightly husky. 'But I do so want to see Marian. It — it's terribly important . . . '

'My daughter is not at home,' said Rayner stiffly.

'So your butler told me. I can't understand it. Did she go away yesterday?'

'She did not.'

'Do you know if she got my letter?'

'I couldn't say.'

The girl moistened her lips with the tip of her tongue and came a little further into the room.

'Do sit down, Mrs. Leyton,' said Heron getting up.

'Thank you.' Rather timidly she sat down in the chair he offered. 'If Marian had got my letter I'm sure she would have wired as I asked her.'

'It shouldn't be difficult to find out,' said Heron. He looked at Rayner. 'Stukes would know, wouldn't he?'

Rayner, his face still set angrily, took the hint and rang the bell. When the butler came the question was put to him.

'Miss Marian received a letter by the second post yesterday, sir,' he said. 'It had a London postmark . . . '

'That would be mine,' said the girl. 'It's not like Marian to have taken no notice . . . '

'We're having a little trouble here this morning,' said Heron. 'Miss Rayner is certainly not at home but we have no idea where she is. She went out last night and hasn't come back.'

The girl's expression changed. The worried look was replaced by one of relief.

'Oh, she did go, then?' she said. 'I'm so glad! I was sure that she wouldn't ignore my letter.'

'She went on your behalf?'

'Yes. I asked her if she could possibly see me for — for a few minutes. I asked her to wire if she couldn't. She didn't wire so I came. But I never saw anything of her . . . '

'Where did you arrange to meet her?' asked Heron.

'In the drive — by the gate. At twelve o'clock last night.' She glanced at Rayner as she spoke but he had gone over to the window and was staring out. There was no need to ask why the appointment had been made for outside the house. Rayner was a stubborn man. He would not have allowed the meeting to take place if he had known about it. The reason for Marian Rayner leaving the house at such a late hour had been cleared up. Except for one thing.

'When you saw Miss Rayner she was crossing the lawn, wasn't she, Farrell?'

'Yes.'

'There's a way round to the end of the drive that way,' grunted Rayner. 'A short cut through the lane.'

'I see.' Obviously Marian Rayner had gone this way in order to avoid the possibility of being seen from Rayner's bedroom, which, Heron discovered later, overlooked the drive. But she had never arrived at the drive gate. What had happened to her?

'Why did you wish to see my daughter?' Rayner turned and faced the girl. 'It seems to me a very strange thing to ask her, to meet you at so late an hour.'

'I — I wanted her to help me.' The girl was embarrassed. She obviously did not want to divulge the reason. Her large eyes looked at them helplessly.

'You go ahead and tell us, dear,' said Thelma. She came over and put her hand on the girl's shoulder. 'Anything you tell us will be treated in confidence, won't it, Felix?'

'Yes, of course.'

'Well, then . . . the — the truth is . . . I've run away from my husband!' The last few words came out in a sudden rush.

Rayner uttered a sound that was completely disapproving.

'It sounds awful, doesn't it? But if you knew — everything — you'd understand. I'm sure you would — all of you. He — he drinks, you see — '

'Did he give you that bruise?' asked Thelma, and she nodded.

'Yes, he gets very violent . . . Marian would have understood. She knew how beastly he was . . . She always wanted me to leave him. But it wasn't easy. You — you see, I have no money of my own. Frank — that's my husband — has sold, or pawned, everything of value that I did have. I was hoping that Marian would . . . Until I could get some kind of job . . . ' By the time she had told them all this her face was scarlet with embarrassment. 'I had to leave him,' she burst out. 'I couldn't stand it any longer . . . '

'You poor child,' said Thelma sympathetically, patting her shoulder. 'Don't you worry any more. You can come and stay at the cottage with us. I'm sure we can do something to help you.'

'It — it's very kind of you,' said the girl huskily, and her eyes filled with tears.

'How did you come to Bishop's Trencham?' asked Heron.

'By train. There's one that gets here at half past eleven. I walked from the station . . . '

'How long did you wait at the drive gate?'

'Until nearly one. I couldn't understand why Marian hadn't come. It was so unlike her . . . '

'What did you do then?'

'I managed to get a room at the inn . . . '

'Had I known about this letter you wrote to my daughter,' said Charles Rayner, 'I should have insisted that my daughter had nothing to do with this matter. I consider that this is an entirely wrong attitude on your part . . . '

'But you can't expect me to go on suffering ill-treatment and worse . . . ?'

'This man is your husband,' said Rayner. 'Whatever he has done your place is with him . . . '

'I think you're being completely unreasonable, Mr. Rayner,' put in Thelma. 'This is none of my business but, really, you appear to be extremely old-fashioned!'

'I'm sorry,' said Rayner stubbornly, 'but my opinion remains unchanged.'

The girl looked at him with troubled eyes.

'I wish I could make you understand,' she said. 'What do you think has happened to Marian?'

'I'm afraid,' said Heron, 'that she has been kidnapped. The whole story is rather a long one. I suggest that you go with my wife. I'll come and see you later. Meanwhile, don't worry. We'll find some way of dealing with your difficulty.'

'Come along, dear,' said Thelma. 'We'll go and get some lunch. I expect you're hungry.'

The girl got up.

'I don't know how I can thank you,' she began.

'Don't try,' said Thelma. 'I'll see you back at the cottage, Felix?'

'Yes, dear,' said her husband.

Thelma said goodbye to the others and went out with the girl.

'I suppose you think I'm a little hard,' said Rayner, after they had gone, 'but I regard marriage very seriously . . . '

'I'd rather not discuss it, if you don't mind,' said Felix Heron. He looked at his watch. 'I'm going to see Miss Lessinger. Perhaps Trench mentioned something to her about this book . . . '

'Can I come with you?' asked Dick.

'Yes, if you want to . . . '

'I was hoping that you'd stay to lunch,' said Rayner.

'Thanks, but I think we ought to get on

with the job,' said Heron. 'Don't worry about your daughter, Mr. Rayner. We'll get her back before she comes to any harm.'

6

1

Dorothy Lessinger lived in a large house on the outskirts of the village. It was a fine old place of weather-beaten stone set in several acres of wooded land. Generations of Lessingers had occupied Abbey Lodge, but with Dorothy, and her brother Alfred, the long line ended. Unless either of them married, which was not unlikely since they were neither of them very old, the estate would pass to a cousin who lived in Australia and would probably sell it.

Dorothy Lessinger was a pleasant-faced, buxom woman, with the healthy, tanned complexion of a life spent mostly in the open air. She affected tweeds, woollen stockings and stout brogues, and her main interests were her horses and the estate.

It had been a surprise to the village

when old Geoffrey Lessinger had left the estate to his daughter instead of to his son. But the estate was not entailed, and Dorothy had always been her father's favourite. Alfred took no interest in hunting or horses. He was a studious type, interested only in old books and his botanical specimens.

The elderly housekeeper admitted Heron and Dick to the huge stone hall, conducted them to the drawing-room, and went to acquaint her mistress that they had called.

They had to wait some little time before Dorothy Lessinger appeared and she was full of apologies.

'I'm so sorry to keep you waiting,' she said with a pleasant smile, 'but I was in the stables with the vet. One of my horses strained a fetlock.'

Heron introduced Dick Farrell and plunged at once into the reason for his visit.

'A book?' Dorothy Lessinger screwed up her face. 'What kind of book?'

'I can't tell you, I'm afraid,' said Heron. 'Percival never mentioned any book to me,' she said. 'It's all very extraordinary, isn't it? Perhaps it's something to do with this man, Rayner.'

'I don't think so,' said Heron. 'It's something concerning Sir Percival Trench.'

'I can't help you,' she said candidly. 'It's all very mysterious. Do you think this murder has anything to do with it? Oh, yes, I've heard all about it. It's the talk of the village!'

'The murder may be mixed up with the rest of it,' said Heron, 'but we've no proof that it is.'

'Rather a coincidence if it isn't,' said Miss Lessinger heartily. 'I wish I could help you about this book but I know nothing about it.'

'It must be of great importance to someone,' said Heron. He told her about the disappearance of Marian Rayner. She was very concerned.

'I've seen her once or twice in the village,' she said. 'She looked quite a nice gel. What are you going to do about it?'

'Do you mean the message that was pinned to the tree?'

She nodded.

'I intend to put a book on the sundial tonight, and see what happens . . . '

'I rather agree with Harry about that,' said Dick. 'It's too obvious a trap.'

'It's worth trying,' said Heron. 'Anyway, we can't ignore the message altogether.'

'I wish I'd questioned Percival about these fears of his more closely,' said Dorothy Lessinger. 'But he was a difficult man to force a confidence from. Will you stay to luncheon? We shall be having ours in half an hour?'

'Thank you, but I don't think I ought to waste the time. I've quite a lot to do . . . '

'Please yourself,' said Miss Lessinger briskly. 'Now, I really must be getting back to the stables . . . '

She broke off as the door opened and a man looked in. He was going with a mumbled apology, when she called him back.

'Come in, Alfred,' she said. 'This is my brother, Mr. Heron.' She introduced them to the newcomer.

He was a tall man, prematurely bald. He had the stooping shoulders of the student, and his clothes hung on his lean figure without any pretentions to fit. His long face was sallow and he peered at them through a pair of spectacles.

'I didn't know you were engaged,' he mumbled.

'We're just going, Mr. Lessinger,' said Heron.

Alfred Lessinger blinked at him nervously.

'Don't let me drive you away,' he said. 'I came to get a book I left in here. Excuse me.'

He began to peer about the room in a short-sighted way as they took their leave of his sister.

'You'll let me know what happens tonight, won't you?' she said.

'Of course,' promised Heron. 'Goodbye for the present.'

'Which way is the post office?' asked Dick as they left the drive of Abbey Lodge.

'Down the hill and turn to the left,' said Heron. 'I'm going back to the cottage.'

He made an appointment to meet Dick at Trencham Close about six o'clock that evening and turned off in the direction of the cottage.

As he strode along his mind was busy with the strange affair in which he had got involved. He shared Harry Glenn's opinion of the outcome of the night's experiment. It was such an obvious trap, but there was just a chance that somebody would fall into it.

He was totally unprepared for what actually did happen.

2

Marian Rayner moved uneasily and a faint moaning sigh escaped her lips. There was pain somewhere, but the mist that drenched her brain had not yet dispersed sufficiently to tell her where.

Vaguely, in that semi-conscious state that was like a partly waking dream, she knew that she was very uncomfortable. An ache seemed to permeate her whole body. Gradually her senses came back and she opened her eyes.

Darkness! A heavy, thick, almost

palpable thing that seemed to be crushing her with a weight of its own. After a little while she began to remember . . .

After saying goodnight to her father and his two guests she had gone upstairs to her room and read again the letter from Isobel Leyton. She had waited until the household was quiet, exchanged her high-heeled shoes for a pair of brogues, and crept down to the back door.

The night was very cold and she shivered a little as she emerged from the warmth of the house. She had been very careful not to make a noise. She had no wish to wake her father. He would be sure to stop her meeting Isobel if he knew.

Once again, as she lay staring into the thick darkness, she remembered crossing the lawn, to the narrow twisting path that led round to the drive. She had been half-way along this path which wound between high clumps of bordering shrubbery, when she had felt the presence of someone near her. There had been a slight rustling of leaves, the breaking of a dry branch, and then a hand had gripped her arm and another had covered her mouth!

A hoarse voice whispered in her ear: 'Make a sound and it'll be your last!' The grip on her arm had relaxed and something hard was thrust into her back.

Again the whisper reached her: 'Attempt to struggle and I'll shoot you dead!'

She had seen nothing of her assailant, only heard that horrible, sibilant whisper.

'Walk!' whispered the voice again. Terrified at the feel of the gun in her spine she had obeyed. He forced her through the thick shrubbery. The branches tore at her dress and stung her face as she stumbled along. In a little while they had reached the slope leading up to the wood. For the first time she was able to catch a glimpse of her captor, but the heavy coat he was wearing rendered him almost shapeless and his face was covered by a muffler, pulled up to the eyes.

She had wondered if they were making for the cottage in the wood, but soon found that they were not. They turned abruptly to the left, following a track along the uneven hillside. Presently, some kind of building loomed up in front of her. The man with her opened a gate and pushed her through. She was shivering with cold and realised that somewhere during that nightmare journey she had lost her scarf. She was propelled across a small, neglected garden to a door in a tumble-down wooden house. She had been pushed through the door into pitch darkness and the door was slammed shut behind her.

A musty odour reached her nostrils, and then she felt his hand on her arm again.

'Wait!' he whispered.

She heard the key turn in a lock and she had been left alone in complete darkness, but not for long. In a few seconds the man came back, carrying a lighted candle and a glass of water. She saw that the room was dirty, draped with cobwebs, and scarcely furnished.

'Drink this,' said the man, still in the same throaty whisper he had used throughout. 'Go on! Do as you're told!'

From beneath his ragged coat he drew a knife. She took the glass with a shaking hand and drank. Almost before she had had time to set the empty glass down, the whole room started to spin dizzily . . . A great veil of darkness had enveloped her and she had remembered nothing more until she had come to her senses a few minutes before.

The pain in her head was agonizing. She tried to move and found that she was helpless. She was lying on something hard and lumpy. It felt like an old mattress. This place to which she had been brought must be fairly near Trencham Close. She reckoned they had walked about two miles. She wondered what time it was but she had no way of finding out. She could hear her watch ticking faintly on her wrist but, of course, she couldn't see it.

She began to wonder who the man was who had forced her to come to this place, and why? From the little she had been able to see of him she concluded that he must be one of the tramps who had been camping out in Denham Wood, but what he wanted with her she could not imagine. And then it came to her. Of course. The book!

That's what he was after! The book! She had no idea what it was or why it was so valuable to someone. She knew no more about it than the smallest child in the village! But it would be difficult to make her captor believe this. Since the book had nothing to do with either herself or her father it must be something concerning Sir Percival Trench.

She tried to figure out what it could be and was still puzzling her still aching head when she fell asleep . . .

She must have slept for a long time because when she awakened suddenly the intense darkness had paled to a cold grey. The morning light was filtering in through chinks in the shutters which had been fastened over the window.

Somewhere in the house she could hear the sound of footsteps and the faint muttering of voices. She couldn't hear anything that was being said but the low mutter went on.

Her mouth and throat were so dry and parched that it was painful to swallow, and she would have given a lot for a glass of water. She tried to call out but she only achieved a husky croak.

The voices had risen. The people,

whoever they were, seemed to be arguing. But they weren't speaking loud enough for her to distinguish what they said.

Abruptly the voices ceased, and she heard a movement. She heard footsteps passing the door, two different sets of footsteps — a firm, heavy tread and a lighter one. There was the click of a latch and the light footsteps went past the window. A door closed, the heavy steps repassed the door, and presently there was silence.

It was some time before any other sound broke the stillness, and then she heard a peculiar noise — a curious intermittent metallic rattling. It stopped just as she realised what it was.

Somewhere near at hand a kettle was boiling furiously! There was a short interval, and then the heavy steps sounded again, but this time they stopped at the door. A key grated in the lock and the man in the ragged coat came in. The muffler was still pulled up over his nose and mouth and he carried a cup of tea in his hand.

'I've brought you some tea,' he said in

his harsh whisper. He came over to the ancient sofa on which she was lying and lifted her until her back was supported against the curving end. He held the cup to her lips and she sipped the steaming tea greedily. It was strong and over-sweet, but to her it was nectar!

When she had emptied the cup he carried it over and set it down on a decrepit table.

'I want to talk to you,' he said. 'You needn't be scared because no harm will come to you, if you do as you're told.'

She looked at him in silence.

'If your father does what he's asked you will be set free,' he said, resting his hands on the table and staring at her over the top of the muffler. 'The time you've got to worry is if he doesn't!'

'If you mean the book,' she said, 'neither my father nor I know anything about it.'

'It's no good lying,' he said sharply.

'I'm not lying!'

'He knows all about it, if you don't,' snapped the man in the ragged coat. 'Don't rely on bluff . . . '

'I give you my word that we neither of us know anything about this book, you're talking about,' she declared. Her voice carried conviction and apparently shook his assurance.

'The book belonged to Sir Percival Trench,' he muttered.

'My father never knew Sir Percival Trench,' she answered. 'We only bought the house . . .'

'With all the contents,' he said quickly. She nodded.

'Yes, that's right.'

'The book I want is *The Sinister Man* . . .'

'By Edgar Wallace?' she broke in.

'You've seen it?' he demanded eagerly.

'Of course, I've read it . . .'

'At Trencham Close?'

'No, I read it when we were abroad . . .'

'The copy I want is in Trencham Close,' he said.

'I don't even know if there is one,' she said. 'If there is I haven't seen it.'

'If you're speaking the truth, young lady,' said the ragged man, 'and your father doesn't know anything about this book, you'd better write him a note and tell him.'

'Why should I?' she said.

'Because, if you don't,' he said, 'I'll hurt you so much that you'll wish you were dead!'

She shrank away from the menace in his voice. It was no idle threat! He meant what he said!

'What do you want me to say?' she whispered huskily.

'That's better!' he answered. 'Write what I tell you and tonight you'll be safe back home . . . '

7

1

When Felix Heron reached the little cottage in the wood he found his wife sipping a cup of coffee in the tiny sitting-room.

'I expect you'd like some lunch,' she said. 'It's all ready for you. Isobel Leyton and I have had ours.'

'Where is she?' he asked.

'Asleep,' replied Thelma. 'She was worn out and I made her go up and lie down. You'll have to be content with a cold meal. I didn't have time to cook anything.'

She went out and came back with a tray containing cold chicken and a salad. Heron poured himself out a John Haig, added a little water, and brought it over to the table where she had set down the tray.

'Any news of Marian Rayner?' asked

his wife as she lit a cigarette and resumed her chair.

He shook his head.

'What do you think Mellins was doing here?' she went on.

'I haven't the faintest idea!' he declared candidly. 'This is turning out to be a more complicated business than I expected.'

'You can say that again!' said Thelma.

'We may have some luck tonight,' said Heron, his mouth full of chicken and salad. 'There's just a chance that we might catch a fish with our bait.'

'You're going to try the book idea?'

He nodded.

'It can't do any harm. I'm rather worried about the girl, though,' she said.

'She won't come to any harm,' he answered confidently.

'But she must be horribly frightened, dear. Where can they have taken her?'

'Not much good speculating, is it?' He drank some whisky and went on with his lunch. 'I'm going to get on the phone to Waldron when I've finished eating. Perhaps he can give me some information about Mellins.'

'Where are you going to phone from?'

'There's a phone at the post-office in the village. It's a call-box. Quite private.'

He finished his lunch and drank the coffee she brought him.

'I'll be off,' he said. 'I shan't be long. I should let that girl sleep as long as she can. She's had a rough time, I think.'

'Yes, I'm rather sorry for her, poor child.'

Half an hour later, Heron was talking to Detective Chief Superintendent Waldron at Scotland Yard, from the call-box at the post office.

'So somebody's got Mellins at last, eh?' said Waldron. 'He's been sticking his neck out for a long time. I'll do what I can to find out what he was doing at — where is it? — Bishop's Trencham. He's got a pal, or used to have, a little 'grass' named Steve Cripps. Slimy little beggar . . .'

'I know him,' said Heron.

'Cripps shopped Johnny Dugan, the peterman. I'll get hold of him and see if he can tell me anything about Mellins. I'll bet if he doesn't know anything he'll soon find out!'

'When can you see him?'

'Might get him tonight. There's a pub in Lambeth where he usually goes.'

'If you get hold of anything will you phone me at this number?' Heron gave the telephone number of Trencham Close. 'I shall be there from six o'clock onwards.'

'What are you up to, eh?' asked Waldron curiously.

'Take too long to tell you now,' said Heron and hung up the receiver. Leaving the post office he walked slowly back to the cottage.

Isobel Leyton was still asleep when he got back. Thelma had washed up the luncheon things and was strolling round the tiny, weed-choked garden. She slipped her arm through Heron's and they entered the cottage.

'What are we going to do about that girl upstairs?' she asked. 'She's had a terrible time with that man she's married to. She's got no parents — they're both dead. We must try and do something for her, Felix.'

'I suppose, she's going to get a

divorce?' he said. 'I could give her an introduction to old Marsden. He's a top-class divorce lawyer . . . '

'And he charges first-class fees!' said Thelma. 'She hasn't any money, darling. Only about six pounds in the world. She wants to get a job . . . '

'That might be fixed up. Can she type?'

'She says she had a very good business education.'

'Well, then it shouldn't be difficult. I could help her there, when we get back to town. In the meanwhile she'd better stay on here. Do you mind?'

'I was going to suggest it . . . '

'Good! I'll still have a word with Marsden. He owes me a good turn for that little business I did for him. He might see this through at a very reduced fee . . . '

She smiled at him affectionately.

'You know,' she said, 'you're a very nice man. I'm glad I married you!'

Isobel Leyton came down to tea, full of apologies for sleeping so long. Heron talked to her about her husband, about a divorce, and about a possible job. She answered sensibly and gratefully.

'It's very kind of you to bother about me,' she said. 'But I'm not going to refuse your help. I really am up against it, but I'll pay you back when I get a job . . . '

'I'll see you do!' he said smiling. 'Meanwhile, don't worry any more. Thelma and I will take care of everything.'

At half past five he left for Trencham Close. As he walked down the hillside he saw with uneasiness that a damp mist was slowly spreading over the countryside. He hoped that it wasn't going to develop into a fog. When he reached the house he found everyone in a state of great excitement.

'Read this!' cried Rayner, thrusting a sheet of paper into his hand. 'The infernal scoundrel! Marian was made to write it . . . '

Heron scanned the letter quickly. It was short:

Dear Father. I am quite safe and I shall remain so if you will put the copy of 'The Sinister Man' by Edgar Wallace,

*on the sundial at midnight tonight. If
you fail I shall be killed. Marian.*

'This is your daughter's writing?' asked
Heron.

'Of course it is!' snapped Rayner. 'They
forced her to write it . . . '

'How did it get here? It didn't come by
post?'

'It was put through the letter-box,' said
Dick.

'Nobody was seen?'

Rayner shook his head.

'Well, we know the book they're after,
that's something,' said Heron. 'Have you
looked for it?'

'We've been through all the books in
the house,' said Harry Glenn. 'There isn't
a copy of *The Sinister Man* among them!'

2

'Well, that's that!' said Felix Heron. 'I
suppose you couldn't have overlooked it?'

'We've searched the entire house,'
declared Dick. 'Every room and every

98

cupboard. It isn't here.'

Heron shrugged his shoulders.

'Well, we'll just have to fall back on the first plan,' he said. 'I wish we could have found the book though. I'd like to have had a look at it.'

'What could there be in the thing?' said Glenn.

'Anything — a message — the key to some kind of code. It's impossible to tell,' said Heron. 'Perhaps some indication of the whereabouts of the missing two hundred and twenty thousand pounds.'

'Good God!' ejaculated Rayner. 'You don't mean it's hidden in the house?'

'No, because I can't imagine any reason why Sir Percival Trench should do such a thing,' answered Heron. 'The money would have been safer in his bank. But something was done with that money. The book may hold the key to whom it was paid, and why.'

'If this book we're going to put on the sundial is found to be a fake,' said Harry Glenn seriously, 'what will happen to Marian?'

That was the thought that was in all

their minds. The girl was in danger once the person, or persons, who held her found that they'd been tricked.

'We've got to see that whoever comes for the book is caught,' said Felix Heron. 'Then we can force him to take us to Miss Rayner.'

'If anything goes wrong?' said Rayner gravely.

'We've got to make certain that it doesn't,' replied Heron.

Thelma put in an appearance just before seven. She had put on a polo-necked sweater and dark slacks ready, as she explained, to help in the night's work.

Rayner suggested a drink before dinner and they went into the dining-room. Thelma had a Dry Fly and the others chose a Gordon's pink gin. Dinner was served at seven-thirty, an excellent meal with which they drank a magnificent burgundy that Rayner told them he had taken over with the rest of the contents of the house. By tacit consent they refrained from discussing the reason for their presence during the meal, but it was in the minds of all of them, particularly

Harry Glenn, who was silent and worried. Dick knew that he was thinking of Marian.

They took coffee in the drawing-room, and Stukes brought in a bottle of Hennessy. When they had finished the coffee and brandy, Felix Heron lit a cigarette.

'Now,' he said, 'let's lay our plans for tonight. We needn't make a move until half past eleven. The letter says midnight. At half past eleven, I suggest that you, Rayner, place a book similar in size to the one they are after on the sundial. Prior to this we will take up our positions in various places nearby from which we can not only see anyone who comes to collect the book, but prevent any possibility of them getting away. Have you any arms in the house?'

'I've my old service revolver,' said Rayner.

'Thelma and I have our own automatics. You two had better arm yourselves with stout sticks. The person we shall be dealing with is likely to be dangerous.'

'He won't stand a chance if I get near him!' said Glenn. 'When I think of that poor girl . . . '

'That's what we've all got to think about,' said Heron. 'Whoever comes must not be allowed to get away . . . '

'You really think that somebody will come?' said Dick dubiously.

'I'm hoping so . . . '

'Well, if they do they must be mad! They might just as well walk into the nearest police station and give themselves up! Surely it must be obvious that we shall be on the watch?'

'Do you know, that's what is worrying me,' said Heron. 'As you say, nobody could be so foolish as to suppose that we shouldn't be watching and waiting. Therefore, this person or persons must be confident that they can get away.'

'And that's the danger,' grunted Glenn.

They discussed the matter from all angles. Rayner had fetched his revolver and methodically cleaned it and oiled it, finally filling all the chambers with cartridges.

At half past ten, Heron went into the library and selected a book that looked suitable, and this he carefully packed in brown paper. Dick and Harry had discovered two heavy sticks in the stand in the hall, thick with massive carved heads, capable of smashing anyone's skull at one blow.

'Now, we'll take up our positions,' said Heron.

They slipped out of the house by the drawing-room window. The white mist that had threatened earlier had not got any thicker, but the night was very cold. There was a chill dampness in the air and they were glad of their overcoats. Charles Rayner stayed behind. He was not due to leave the house until half past eleven when he would ostentatiously carry the parcelled book to the rose garden and put it on the old sundial.

The rose garden lay at the side of the house. Four shallow steps led down to it and a low wall surrounded the whole place. Ornamental bushes grew in large tubs at intervals round the rectangle and behind two of these, Heron stationed Glenn and Farrell.

'Do nothing until I call to you,' he warned. 'I shall wait until the person we are expecting has actually picked up the book. When I give the signal close in on him.'

'He won't get away, I promise you,' grunted Glenn.

'We daren't let him!' said Heron. 'Come on, Thelma, we'll go over here.'

They went over to the other side of the rose garden and concealed themselves behind two similar tubs.

'We can do nothing now but wait,' whispered Heron.

'I hope it isn't a very long one,' said his wife. 'This is not my idea of a pleasant way to spend an evening!'

The whole garden was damp and chill. The drops of condensed moisture dripped from the leaves with a monotonous plop, plop. But for that they might have been in a dead world, a garden of ghosts.

Slowly the minutes passed. Thelma was getting chilled to the bone in spite of her thick, black pullover. To add to her discomfort she began to feel a twinge of cramp. The time crept on. Presently they heard the sound of footsteps crunching on gravel.

'That's Rayner,' whispered Heron as he

felt his wife stiffen.

The firm steps came nearer. A blot of shadow appeared at the top of the shallow steps and passed them as Rayner walked over to the sundial. It was so dark that they couldn't distinguish any detail, he was just a shadow among shadows.

He paused at the sundial, and Heron guessed that he was putting the book down on the dial. After a moment he moved away and retraced his steps. The crunching of the gravel under his feet sounded for a minute and then all was silence once more.

Heron looked at the illuminated dial of his watch. It was just half past eleven!

The half-hour that followed was endless, or seemed so to the watchers.

A quarter to twelve . . . ten minutes to . . . five minutes to . . .

Midnight!

A clock in the village struck the hour faintly. At any moment now the person they were waiting for should put in an appearance . . .

But there was no sound! No movement!

Nothing broke the silence of the dripping garden!

Five leaden minutes dragged by. Ten minutes. And still nothing happened!

Thelma stretched one leg cautiously to relieve the stiffness of her cramped muscles. Heron remained rigid, alert and watchful.

Twenty past twelve ... Half past twelve ...

Had the trap been suspected after all? Was their vigil to be for nothing ... ?

A faint sound reached them — a curious, scraping sound. It came from somewhere in the darkness of the garden. Somebody was clambering over the low wall!

Thelma laid her hand on his arm. Peering in the direction from which the faint sounds had come, they saw the mist darken and a shadow loomed, vague and unsubstantial, curiously distorted ...

It crept, a shapeless blot, towards the sundial in the centre of the rose garden. Heron's hand dropped to his pocket and his fingers closed over the butt of his automatic.

The shadow was at the sundial now ...

'Right!' Felix Heron's voice rang out, clear and staccato in the silence.

The shadow by the sundial seemed to elongate and break up. Heron, with Thelma just behind him, raced towards it. Dick and Glenn came running from the opposite direction . . .

A shot rang out! There was a scream, a high-pitched scream, and the shadow by the sundial crumpled up and fell, sprawling.

Heron flashed the torch he had pulled out of his pocket on the prone figure. The man had fallen on his face and a pool of blood was forming on the stone paving beneath the head. The shabby hat had fallen off and the ragged coat was hunched up about the shoulders.

Heron bent down and gently turned the limp body over. A muffler covered the face, and blood was welling from the side of the neck.

'Who is it?' asked Thelma.

Heron pulled the muffler away from the face, flooding it with the light from his torch.

The dead man was Alfred Lessinger!

8

1

The man was without his spectacles but there could be little doubt of his identity.

'But I don't understand,' said Dick. 'Alfred Lessinger — that's Miss Lessinger's brother . . . '

Felix Heron nodded.

'That's right,' he said. 'I can't understand it, either . . . '

'Who shot him?' asked Thelma.

'I wish I could tell you, dear,' said her husband. He broke off as hurried footsteps sounded on the gravel and Charles Rayner joined them.

'What's happened?' he demanded. 'I heard the sound of the shot . . . '

Heron quickly explained.

'Miss Lessinger's brother!' ejaculated Rayner. 'Do you mean the woman who was engaged to Trench?'

'Yes,' said Heron. 'Look, we can't stand

here discussing this. Murder has been done. You'd better telephone the police.'

Reluctantly Rayner went off to telephone.

'Did you see where that shot came from?' Heron asked his wife.

'Over there — from just beyond the wall,' she answered and pointed. 'I saw the flash . . .'

'You two stay here, will you?' said Heron. 'Come on, dear. Let's see if we can find anything of the shooter.'

At the spot by the wall which Thelma had indicated they found several smudged footprints.

'That's where he stood waiting,' muttered Heron. 'He must've been there soon after we took up our positions in the rose garden.'

'Who could it have been?'

'Don't ask me! I haven't the least idea. The whole thing is getting too complicated . . .'

'What are we going to do about Marian Rayner? We still don't know where she is.'

'I know,' said Heron, a little irritably. 'You don't have to tell me! Come on, we'll go back. There's nothing we can do here.'

They returned to Farrell and Glenn by the body.

'Did you find anything?' asked Dick.

'Nothing of any account. There are traces of footprints . . . '

Rayner came hurrying back.

'I've phoned the police,' he said. 'I've been thinking. Can these Lessingers be at the bottom of all this?'

'It was Miss Lessinger who came to me,' said Heron.

'That could've been a blind . . . '

'It could have been but I don't think it was.'

'Her brother could have been mixed up in it without his sister knowing, couldn't he?' suggested Dick.

'What about Marian?' interrupted Harry Glenn. 'We must do something about finding her . . . '

'What?' demanded Heron.

'I don't know, but she's still in great danger,' said Glenn. 'This man who shot Lessinger — he may carry out that threat to kill her . . . '

'It wouldn't serve any purpose,' said Heron. 'She's useless to them dead.'

'Well, here's the fake book,' said Dick. 'I picked it up when it dropped from Lessinger's hand.'

'It didn't do us much good, did it?' grunted Glenn.

'We couldn't foresee that someone was going to shoot the man who came to collect it,' snapped Heron.

The arrival of Inspector Trafford, obviously roused from his bed, put an end to any further discussion.

'What's this I'm told?' he asked. 'Somebody been shot?'

When he was told what had happened, he frowned.

'Mr. Lessinger, eh? What was he doing in the garden at this time of night, eh?'

At Felix Heron's further explanation his frown deepened.

'I should have been told about all this,' he said portentously. 'If I'd have been here, things might have been different.'

'What else would you have done?' asked Heron.

'I know my job!' said Trafford. 'I

shouldn't have let Mr. Lessinger be murdered under my very eyes!'

'You'd have jumped forward and caught the bullet before it could hit him, I suppose?' said Dick.

The inspector regarded him with disapproval.

'This is not the time to be funny!' he said. 'Will you look at the body, doctor?'

The doctor, the same man who had come with him in the case of Mellins, stepped forward and knelt by the dead man. His examination was brief.

'The bullet entered the throat just under the jawbone,' he announced. 'It severed the jugular and lodged in the right shoulder. Death was practically instantaneous. I'll let you have the bullet after the P.M.'

He rose to his feet and Trafford took his place. A quick search revealed that all the pockets were empty.

'Has Miss Lessinger been informed?' he asked, looking up.

'No, not yet,' answered Heron.

Inspector Trafford got heavily to his feet.

'That had better be attended to at once,' he said.

'I'll telephone her,' said Rayner.

'Now, I should like to inspect these footprints,' said Trafford. 'They might tell me a lot.'

He inspected the marks with great importance.

'Obviously a heavily built man,' he remarked.

'Those prints you are looking at are mine!' said Heron. 'I made them when I climbed over the wall.'

'You should have been more careful!' grunted the inspector. He measured the smudges carefully, noted the result in his note-book, and pursed his rather thick lips. 'Now, I'd better see the servants,' he said.

'The servants were all in bed . . . '

'I follow routine in these matters,' said Trafford. He called to the constable he had brought with him. 'Go and fetch an ambulance. I'll be here when you get back.'

'I'll come with you,' said the thin doctor. 'Nothing for me to do here.'

113

As they started for the house, leaving Dick to stay with the body, they heard the police car going down the drive. And then, Heron heard something else, and stopped.

'What is it?' asked Trafford.

'Listen!'

Faintly to their ears came the sound of running steps, hurried, uneven, stumbling steps, as though the runner were in the last stage of exhaustion. They came from the direction of the drive.

'Who is it?' asked Glenn, but before anyone could answer him he saw for himself. He was just in time to catch Marian Rayner as she fell exhausted into his arms.

2

They carried the unconscious girl into the drawing-room and laid her on the settee. Charles Rayner fetched a bottle of Hennessy, poured out some brandy and made her swallow a few drops. Her face was pale and covered with streaks of dirt.

Her hands were scratched and raw and there was a jagged cut on one of her wrists. Her hair hung in damp wisps about her face, and the thin dress she was wearing was soaked.

The effect of the brandy was almost instantaneous. She sighed and her eyes flickered. When she saw Heron bending over her she tried to struggle up with a stifled cry.

'It's all right, Marian,' said Rayner, coming forward. 'You're safe — at home. Drink a little more of this,' he held the glass of Hennessy out and she took it, sipping the spirit gratefully.

'Do you feel strong enough to tell us what happened?' asked Heron.

'She ought to go straight to bed,' said Thelma.

'I should be glad,' put in Inspector Trafford, who had watched the proceedings with a glowering face, 'if the young lady would make a statement at once . . . '

'She'll make a statement when she's well enough!' snapped her father.

'I'm quite all right,' said Marian. She drank the remainder of the brandy, and

Glenn took the glass and put it down. 'I'll tell you the whole story.'

Inspector Trafford produced his notebook and took voluminous notes as she related what had happened to her.

'After I'd written that letter,' she continued, 'the man didn't treat me at all badly. He gave me a good meal, watching me while I ate and retying my hands afterwards. I fell asleep during the afternoon and it was dark when I awoke. This time a candle had been left so that I could see. There was no sound in the place and it suddenly occurred to me that if I'd been left alone, perhaps I could escape.

'I tried to loosen the cords that bound my wrists, but they'd been tied too tightly. They'd been bound behind my back, which made it more difficult. And then I saw that the plate on which my meal had been brought was still on the table. I remembered some of the thrillers I'd read and seen on the telly. I thought if I could reach the plate and break it I might be able to cut through the cords at my wrists.

'I rolled off the old sofa and managed to reach the table. The plate had been left quite near the edge and I banged myself up against the table, rocking it in the hope that the plate would slide off on to the floor. It did eventually, but it didn't break! You've no idea how long it took me to break that plate!' She smiled up at them and went on: 'I did it at last and managed to get one of the pieces between my fingers. But I found that I couldn't reach the cords! For a long time I lay on the floor wondering what I could do. I was terrified that the man might come back.

'And then I got an idea! The boards of the floor were old and badly fitting. There was a place where I managed to wedge the broken bit of the plate. It fitted quite tightly, jammed up against one of the beams. I began to rub the cords up and down against the sharp edge. It cut my wrist and scratched my hands, but at last one of the cords gave. Just as it did so the candle went out!

'It didn't take long after that to get my ankles free, and I wasted no time in getting out of the horrible place. The door was locked but the shutters over the window were only secured by a bar. I soon had them open, unlatched the window and climbed out. It was pitch dark and rather misty, but I didn't care about that! All I wanted to do was to get home! Luckily I remembered the way we'd come and I ran! I don't think I've ever run so hard!'

'Thank God, you're back!' said Rayner.

'That cottage you were taken to, miss,' said Trafford, 'has been empty for years. It belongs to Miss Lessinger . . . '

'What was the man like — the man at this place you were taken to?' asked Heron.

'I never saw him, not his face. He kept a muffler over it. But he looked like a tramp, dirty and ragged . . . '

'Now, you're going to bed!' insisted Thelma. 'You need lots of rest after what you've been through . . . '

They saw the question in the girl's eyes as she looked at Thelma, and Rayner introduced them. Marian wanted to hear more about the book but they persuaded her to go to bed at last. Thelma took her up and agreed to tell her what had happened that night while she got undressed and had a hot bath.

'Did you tell Miss Lessinger about her brother?' asked Inspector Trafford, after Marian had gone. Rayner shook his head.

'I tried to get through but there was no reply,' he said. 'I'll go and try again.'

He went out, and Trafford consulted his notes.

'This is a very strange business,' he said. 'I don't get the hang of it at all.'

'I should have thought that a man of your experience, inspector, would have found it quite clear!' said Heron.

Inspector Trafford was immune to sarcasm. It passed completely over his head.

'There's something I don't know about,' he said suspiciously. 'I want a lot more information . . . '

He broke off as Rayner came back, his face the picture of astonishment.

'I wish you'd come to the phone, Heron,' he said. 'I can't understand it . . . '

'What's the matter?' asked Heron. 'Did you get through to Abbey Lodge.'

'I did,' said Rayner. 'I got through, and the man who answered the phone was Alfred Lessinger!'

9

1

Inspector Trafford's eyes bulged until he looked like a red-faced golliwog.

'It can't be,' he said.

'I'll come,' said Heron. He followed Rayner into the library and picked up the receiver which lay on the writing-table.

'Hello!' he called.

'Is th-that Mr. Rayner,' came a faint voice.

'Who is that speaking?'

'Alfred Lessinger. What's the matter?'

'I can't explain over the phone,' said Heron. 'Can we come round?'

'Now?' The voice sounded surprised. 'It's v-very late . . . '

'I know, but the matter is urgent. A man has been killed . . . '

'Hold on a m-moment, will you?'

'Yes.' Heron turned to the puzzled Rayner. 'That was Lessinger, without a doubt. He's gone to wake his sister . . . '

'Then the man who was shot must be someone else,' said Inspector Trafford, who had followed them to the library.

'Obviously!' said Heron. He turned again to the telephone as the clear, business-like voice of Dorothy Lessinger came over the line.

'Is that Mr. Heron? My brother says you wish to see me at once?'

'Yes, it's rather urgent.'

'Come over at once, then,' she said crisply.

'I'll drive you over,' said Rayner, as Heron put down the receiver.

'I'll come, too,' said Trafford. 'It seems to me there are a lot of things that want looking into, eh?'

Charles Rayner brought the car round and they set off for Abbey Lodge, after the inspector had left a note for the constable when he returned with the ambulance.

As they came up the drive of Abbey Lodge they saw a dim light shining through the glass panels of the front entrance, and Rayner had scarcely stopped the car when the main door opened and Dorothy Lessinger came forward to greet them.

'Come in,' she said. 'I've just made some coffee; I expect you'll be glad of something of the sort.' She shivered and closed the door quickly.

She hadn't waited to dress but had slipped on a fleecy woollen dressing-gown which enveloped her stout, homely figure. She took them into the big drawing-room, and a man who had been huddled in an easy chair, also clad in a dressing-gown, rose to his feet.

If was Alfred Lessinger. There was no doubt.

Felix Heron introduced Charles Rayner, and Miss Lessinger busied herself with the coffee.

'Now, what's all this about?' she asked as she handed it round. 'Why did you want to see me at this hour of the morning?'

Heron explained, and her eyes were round and astonished when he had finished.

'You say this man is like Alfred?'

'He's exactly like your brother, miss,' said Trafford, pushing himself a little forward. 'As like as two peas.'

'Extraordinary!' She frowned. 'I wonder who it could be?'

'Have you any relations?' asked Heron, and she shook her head.

'We've no relations at all, except an aunt who lives abroad,' she said. 'Really, I can't make it out at all. Do you think this man can have had anything to do with Sir Percival's death?'

'What is this about Sir Percival Trench's death?' inquired Inspector Trafford heavily.

Dorothy Lessinger's eyes met Heron's.

'I think I'd tell the inspector,' he said.

'I agree with you, Mr. Heron,' she said. 'The fact is, inspector, I am not, and never have been satisfied, that Sir Percival's death was an accident.'

Trafford looked as if he'd been stung.

'What's that, eh? Not an accident? But that was the verdict of the coroner's jury, miss, eh?'

'I know, but it never convinced me!' declared Miss Lessinger firmly. 'I believe that Sir Percival was murdered! That's why I went to Mr. Heron . . . '

'If you had any grounds for thinking this, and it's a very serious statement to make, eh?' commented the inspector, 'you should have come to me. I was the right person to be told about it, eh?'

'I wanted to avoid unpleasant publicity until I had more to go on,' she answered. 'Mr. Heron agreed to look into the matter for me, and . . . '

'Discovered that there was probably a great deal in your suspicions,' said Heron.

'I should have been told about all this,' said the inspector. 'I shall make it my business to mention the fact that I was not informed about any of this when I make my report.'

'You were informed that Miss Rayner had disappeared,' snapped Heron, who was losing patience with Inspector Trafford, 'and you refused to take the matter seriously, suggesting that she had run off with some man or other. Put that in your report, too!'

Trafford's face assumed a beautiful plum colour.

'I shall put in my report whatever I consider necessary!' he retorted. 'I think that a lot of people have been withholding valuable evidence!'

Alfred Lessinger moved a little closer to them.

'Why w-was this man shot?' he asked.

'I don't know,' said Heron. 'The man who was killed in the rose garden at Trencham Close was the same man who kidnapped Miss Rayner. Why he should have been shot and who shot him is a complete puzzle.'

'Like the secret of the book,' put in Rayner. 'It's not at the house . . . '

'Unless Percival hid it,' said Dorothy Lessinger. 'Don't you think that this book could have a connection with the disappearance of all this money?'

'It's more than likely,' agreed Heron.

'I've been thinking about it all day,' she went on, 'and I wonder if we've been wrong in supposing that he paid this money away. Couldn't he have drawn it out and hidden it somewhere?'

'Why? Why should he do such a thing?'

'Was Sir Percival, you'll forgive me for asking,' said Rayner, 'was he eccentric?'

She smiled.

'He had his own ideas about things,' she said. 'But — well, no. I wouldn't call him eccentric in the way you mean.'

'If — if I might make a s-suggestion,' said Alfred Lessinger diffidently. 'There's a possible explanation.'

Felix Heron turned to him quickly.

'Go on, Mr. Lessinger,' he said.

'If Percival was afraid that his fortune might be c-confiscated he might have drawn it out of the bank to ensure that it was safe.'

'Confiscated?'

'I wonder if you're right, Alfred!' exclaimed his sister. 'Do you know I never thought of that!'

'Why was he afraid that his fortune might be confiscated?' asked Heron.

'It was his firm conviction that the country was going bankrupt!' said Dorothy Lessinger. 'He was very worried about it. He used to say that successive inept governments had brought it to the verge of ruin. His argument was that the country was no longer controlled by any government but by the trade unions. In his opinion continually increased wage demands, less working hours, strikes, and the present trend of laziness and apathy, was bound to lead to economic chaos.'

Felix Heron looked thoughtful.

'I see,' he remarked. 'I wish I'd known this before.'

'I never thought it was important,' she said.

'There was a great d-deal of s-sense in his reasoning. All these t-temporary measures will not effect a c-cure, you know,' said Alfred Lessinger. 'Only a drastic reorganization of the present labour problems will effect a p-permanent c-cure . . .'

'It seems to me,' broke in Inspector Trafford impatiently, 'that we're wasting time, eh? All this conjecturing and theorizing isn't getting us anywhere, eh? What we want is facts, eh?'

'I shall be interested to see you collect some!' said Heron.

Trafford cleared his throat. He took out his inevitable note-book.

'Perhaps, Miss Lessinger,' he said, 'you wouldn't mind answering a few questions, eh?'

'Just a minute,' said Heron.

Trafford glared at him.

'I'll trouble you not to interrupt me,' he said.

'I want to make a suggestion,' answered Heron. 'It will probably appeal to you, inspector.'

'What is this suggestion, eh?' grunted Trafford ungraciously. 'I warn you that I'll not stand for much more interference, eh?'

'Take the finger-prints of the dead man,' said Heron, 'and send them up to C.R.O. at Scotland Yard. Whatever the answer is you'll have what you're looking for — a fact!'

2

The dawn was breaking when Felix Heron and Rayner left Abbey Lodge, a cold, sickly grey light that struggled through the thin mist and made the gaunt trees and dripping hedges look as though they had been smudged in with a sooty finger on ground glass.

Inspector Trafford had left earlier after

a meticulous questioning of the Lessingers. Most of the questions he asked were quite irrelevant and got him very little further than when he started.

Heron's suggestion regarding the dead man's fingerprints had been something of a bow at a venture. He thought it very probable that it might lead to his identity. Since he was obviously a crook of some kind it was possible that he had passed through the hands of the police. In any event it would do no harm.

As soon as they got back to Trencham Close they inquired after Marian Rayner. Thelma, who was still there, told them that she was sleeping peacefully.

The body of the unknown man had been removed from the rose garden and both Dick Farrell and Harry Glenn were still up. Heron found them dozing in front of the library fire, but ready to hear what had happened at Abbey Lodge. He told them as shortly as possible.

'I'm going to have a look at that cottage where Miss Rayner was taken, as soon as it's quite light,' he ended. 'Do you want to come with me?'

They both wanted to come. Heron wanted his wife to stay with Charles Rayner until they came back, but she objected.

'What about that girl, Mrs. Leyton?' she asked. 'She's all alone up at the cottage. Don't you think I ought to go and see if she's all right?'

'I'd forgotten that,' said Heron. 'All right, you come with us. We all go in that direction.'

They followed the same route that Dick and Glenn had taken on the morning when they had found the body of Mellins swinging from the tree. Thelma left them, however, soon after they reached it, continuing on to the cottage while they turned off along the hillside.

The mist had thinned a little but it was still thick in the hollows. Eventually they reached the tumble-down cottage to which Marian had been taken.

It was a desolate place enough, hidden by a belt of trees. The small garden was overrun with weeds and filled with heaps of rubbish, relics of the last tenant's departure. The building was in an advanced state of dilapidation. A wooden porch over the door hung drunkenly awry, many of the windows were broken, and there were great cracks in the plaster.

Felix Heron tried the door, but it was locked and so was the back entrance. They found the window through which Marian had escaped, and were able to get in that way.

The window was a small one and very little light found its way into the room which at one time had evidently been the main living-room of the cottage.

The low ceiling was blackened with age, and there was dust everywhere. The ancient, horse-hair covered sofa was dropping to pieces, and the table was in little better condition. On the centre table was an old beer bottle in which was stuck a guttered end of candle.

Scattered on the floor were the bits of the plate which the girl had broken in her successful attempt to escape. The floor was thick with dust and they could see where she had crawled from the sofa to the table. There were other footprints, too.

With a warning to Farrell and Glenn to

keep near the window, Heron made a search of the place. As near as he could judge the footprints in the dust corresponded roughly with the shape of the shoes the dead man had been wearing. They were definitely smaller and neater than the prints left by the man who had shot him.

The door of the room was locked, but the old wood was rotten and a sharp thrust from his shoulder burst the door open. Beyond was a narrow passage, so dark that he had to switch on his torch.

It ran apparently from the front to the back of the cottage. Here again there was dust everywhere. As he put his light on the bare boards he saw a further jumble of footprints.

This time there were two sets. The second set had been made by a shoe exactly similar to those worn by the man who had fired the fatal shot from the wall of the rose garden. There was no mistaking that wide, broad-toed mark. It was identical!

There were no other prints and Heron picked his way along the passage towards the back. There was a door, partly open, which led to a kitchen, even dustier and dirtier than the living-room. There was rubbish and grease everywhere. A tray containing the remains of a meal stood on a bench under the window. A kettle and a dirty frying-pan were on the hearth by the rusty old range, and near them was a spirit-stove.

Several cigarette ends lay scattered about the filthy floor. Heron picked one up. It was of the cheaper brand that can be bought anywhere. His search was not entirely without result, however, though at the time he failed to see the significance of his discovery.

On one corner of the built-in dresser he found a hair. It was a dark-brown hair and near it were several more. He picked them up carefully. They were greasy with some kind of hair cream, and the ends were split.

Heron put them in an old envelope he had in his pocket. There was nothing else in the kitchen to interest him and he went back along the passage and ascended the narrow stairs to the rooms above.

There were two of these. They were both completely empty and a smooth grey film of dust covered the bare boards. Evidently neither of the people who had been using the cottage had come up here. They hadn't lived here. They had just made use of the place and obviously lived elsewhere.

Heron rejoined the others and told them what he had found.

'We may as well have a look at the garden before we go back,' he concluded. 'I don't expect we shall find anything.'

There wasn't anything and they left, Dick and Glenn to return to Trencham Close, and Felix Heron to go back to his own cottage.

He found his wife in the kitchen making coffee.

'Well, how did you get on?' she asked, taking the percolator off the stove and putting in on a tray. 'Come and have some coffee in the sitting-room. There's a fire there.'

'How's Mrs. Leyton?' he asked.

'She woke up when I came in,' said Thelma. 'I gave her some coffee and she's gone to sleep again. She's suffering from acute nervous exhaustion, poor child.' She poured out the coffee. 'I told her that Marian Rayner was all right. She wants to see her.'

She gave him his coffee and sat down. 'Now, tell me all the latest news,' she said.

He told her about Sir Percival Trench's fear concerning his money if the country's economy should collapse.

'I'll bet that's it,' she said, when he had finished. 'That money is at the bottom of it. He's hidden it somewhere . . . '

'That doesn't make sense,' said her husband. 'If his fears were realized the money would still be valueless, wouldn't it? Just so much waste paper. If he did anything like that he must have converted it into something that would retain its value whatever happened to the currency of the country . . . '

'Like diamonds or something similar?' she inquired.

He nodded.

'He must have had a bee in his bonnet,' said Thelma.

'I'm not so sure,' said Heron. 'What he feared *could* happen, you know. Unless the people pull their socks up and really get down to hard work, it might happen quite easily. Strikes and wage demands have forced prices up. The export market, on which we depend, is suffering and will continue to suffer. Nobody seems to have sense enough to see that the only way to get back to prosperity is to produce more goods at the right price . . . '

'And the right quality,' put in Thelma. 'The stuff that is being made these days is terrible! Shoddy, that's all you can call it.'

'It's a shoddy age!' remarked Heron, shaking his head. 'Shoddy is a description that applies to nearly everything. Shoddy behaviour, shoddy morals, shoddy dress. The theatres are full of shoddy plays. There is shoddy entertainment on television and in the cinema. Shoddy music, twanged and bawled by groups of shoddy teenagers. Shoddy paintings, shoddy buildings, shoddy furniture, shoddy critics, shoddy standards in everything. The quality has gone from life, the quality that made British craftsmanship sought after all over the world. All that's left is a shoddy country misgoverned by shoddy politicians with shoddy ideas!'

'Well!' Thelma stared at her husband. 'I'd no idea you felt so strongly about it!'

'It's a pity there aren't more people who feel as I do! Something might be done to stop the rot! But most people are too apathetic and complacent! There's nobody to wake them up, nobody to tell them that they're sliding into an abyss! There isn't one member of any of the political parties with an original idea! No wonder Sir Percival Trench was worried.'

'What you need,' declared Thelma, 'is a good breakfast and some sleep . . . '

'I'll have the breakfast but not the sleep,' said Heron. 'I'm going to tackle this business from a new angle. I'm going up to London.'

'When?'

'There's a train at eight-fifteen. You can stay down here and keep an eye on things. But be careful. I shall be back tomorrow, I hope.'

After a good breakfast, Heron set off for the station. He was very tired but he decided that he could get a nap on the train.

The first thing he did when he reached his flat in Park Lane was to put through a call to Waldron.

'Hello,' said the Chief Superintendent. 'Where are you phoning from?'

'I'm at home. Came up this morning. Did you get hold of Cripps?'

'No. I tried all his usual haunts but nobody's seen him for several days. I've got a look-out being kept for him. How are you getting on with the Mellins business?'

'Nothing, so far. There was another murder last night.' He told Waldron what had happened in the rose garden at Trencham Close. 'This man Trafford is sending the dead man's finger-prints up for possible identification. I'd like to know the result.'

'I'll come round,' said Waldron. 'How long are you staying at the flat?'

'That depends. Certainly until tomorrow.'

'I'll drop in some time this evening. It may be a bit late . . . '

'Don't worry about that. I shall be glad

to see you any time.'

'Right you are, then. In the meanwhile, I'll see what I can get hold of.'

Waldron rang off. Heron frowned as he put the receiver back on its rack. Why had Stephen Cripps, the little 'grass' disappeared? Was there any connection between this and the murder of Mellins, the informer? They had been friends. Did Cripps know what Mellins had known?

He broke off his conjectures as his secretary came in. He was an ugly man, middle-aged, and bald. He looked large and clumsy but he could type accurately at great speed, and his huge hands had an extraordinarily delicate touch.

'Hello,' he exclaimed in surprise. 'I didn't know you'd come back.'

'I've only just arrived, Harry,' said Heron. That was the only name this efficient secretary bore. If he had any other it was never mentioned by anyone. 'Where've you been?'

'To the post. There's a lot of stuff you ought to see . . .'

'It'll have to wait. Can't you deal with it?'

'Most of it,' said Harry. 'There are one or two letters you'll have to deal with yourself.'

'All right,' said Heron. 'Pour me out a large pink gin and I'll look at 'em.'

Harry went over to the cocktail cabinet, took out a bottle of Gordon's gin, and manufactured the drink with the deftness of an expert barman. He brought it over to his employer with a small jug of water and set it down on the desk at which Heron had seated himself.

'Thanks,' said Heron. He added a little water and took a drink.

'Those are the letters — on the blotting-pad,' said Harry. 'You'll see why I can't deal with them when you read them.'

'Will you phone down to Mancini's and ask them to send up a tournedos steak, sauté potatoes and fresh peas, oh, and mushrooms. A piece of ripe camembert and crackers.'

Harry nodded.

While he was gone to phone from his own office, Heron hastily read through the letters. When the secretary came back

141

he dictated replies, finished his pink gin, and sat back with a sigh of relief. In his mind he ran over a résumé of the case. It was a queer business. Had Sir Percival converted his money to something that he considered safer? Had he hidden whatever this was, in the house? And was the hiding place mentioned in the book which these unknown people were so anxious to get hold of? It was a possible and plausible solution, but how had they become aware of the existence of this — treasure for want of a better name — in the first place?

The arrival of a waiter with his lunch broke into Felix Heron's thoughts. It was meticulously served and cooked. Mancini catered for people who understood good food and he always gave his very best attention to any order from Heron. He had once been able to do the stout little Italian a service and Mancini had never forgotten it.

Heron enjoyed his lunch and made himself some black coffee with which he drank some Hennessy brandy. Lighting a cigarette he put through a telephone call to Trencham Close and asked to speak to Dick Farrell.

'Listen, Farrell,' he said. 'You've got around among a lot of crooks, working for that newspaper of yours. Have you ever come in contact with a chap named Stephen Cripps or Steve Cripps?'

'No, I don't think so. What's his line?'

'Well, he's not exactly a crook. He's more of a 'grass' . . . '

'Like Mellins, do you mean?'

'Yes, they were pals. Cripps has deserted his usual haunts, apparently, and I was wondering if he might not have meandered to the neighbourhood of Bishop's Trencham. Look, Thelma knows him — at least she knows what he looks like. Ask her to keep a look out.'

'She's just collected Marian and taken her along to see Mrs. Leyton,' said Dick. 'I'll go and tell her what you say.'

'How did Rayner take that?'

'He wasn't at all sold on the idea, but he didn't say anything. When are you coming back?'

'Tomorrow, I hope,' said Heron, 'if I can get through all I want to do.'

'Don't overdo it!' said Dick. 'Seen my stuff in the *Messenger*? Front page an' all!'

'I hope you've been discreet.'

'Don't worry. I'm a master at saying nothing in a dramatic and interesting way!' retorted Dick.

Heron rang off and told Harry to bring the car round. He was feeling horribly tired, with that hot and pricking sensation of the eyes which is a sign of lack of sleep, but he could not afford the time to take a rest.

He drove to the offices of the late Sir Percival's solicitors. Messrs. Sedman and Marks occupied the first floor of an old-fashioned house in Great James' Street. He was only kept waiting a few minutes before the elderly clerk returned to say that Mr. Sedman would see him.

The lawyer was a big, bluff, hearty man, quite unlike the usual run of solicitors, and he greeted Heron with a genial smile from behind his big desk. Here there was no accumulation of dusty papers, bundles of red-taped documents, and the usual musty atmosphere that is generally associated with the offices of the legal profession.

Mr. Sedman evidently believed in neatness. Everything had a place and everything was in that place. The rows of black japanned deed-boxes that lined one wall were as clean as when they had left the makers. The top of the desk was the acme of tidiness with only those bare essentials which Mr. Sedman was requiring at the moment.

The lawyer shook hands with Heron and, almost in the same movement, waved him to a large leather armchair facing the desk.

'Perhaps you would care to try one of these cigars, sir?' he said. 'They were presented to me by a client whose business concerns these things. I can strongly recommend them.'

He pulled open a drawer and produced a cedarwood box which he pushed across the desk.

Heron selected one of the long cigars and sniffed it appreciatively. The genial lawyer watched him at he lit it carefully.

'Delightful!' he commented, slowly

expelling a little cloud of fragrant smoke.

Mr. Sedman's fat face creased into a pleased smile.

'I thought them very good,' he said. 'Cigars are a weakness of mine. Now, what have you come to see me about?'

'The same thing that I came to see you about before. Sir Percival Trench.'

'I rather expected you. I've read the newspapers. You have been having a great deal of excitement at Bishop's Trencham?'

'Quite considerable. Last night there was another murder . . . '

He explained what had happened in the rose garden. Mr. Sedman listened gravely.

'Most extraordinary, most extraordinary!' he commented. 'I fail to see how I can help you. I told you everything I could when you called before.'

'Nothing fresh has occurred to you since?'

Mr. Sedman shook his head.

'I'm afraid not. I have thought over the matter but I can recollect nothing about my late client that would give you any further information . . . '

'The whole thing hinges on this money. I'm inclined to reconsider my original opinion that Sir Percival was being blackmailed. I think he drew out this large sum for a purpose of his own.'

'What purpose?' asked Mr. Sedman.

Heron examined the ash on the end of his cigar.

'I've learned from Miss Lessinger that he was worried about the state of the country.'

'Aren't we all?' Mr. Sedman made a grimace.

'Naturally. But Sir Percival was, apparently, obsessed with the idea that all money might become valueless if the economic situation of the country grew worse and finally collapsed.'

Mr. Sedman pursed his lips and gently massaged his fleshy chin.

'Sir Percival certainly *was* rather worried about the economic situation,' he agreed. 'He had no confidence in the Government, or the Opposition, for that matter. His opinion was that they were quite incapable. 'A lot of incompetent noodles' were the words he used.'

Heron laughed.

'I'm rather inclined to agree with him!' he said. 'However, what I'm getting at is this: feeling as strongly as he did, isn't it likely that he drew out this money and converted it to something that would prove more concrete in the event of an economic collapse?'

Mr. Sedman considered this.

'It is possible,' he said. 'You mean some form of collateral that would retain its value whatever happened to the finances of the country?'

'Exactly!'

'And that he hid this in, or near, Trencham Close?'

Heron nodded.

'That's my idea.' He told the lawyer about the book. 'The book holds the secret of the hiding-place. Do you agree?'

'Well, there's no proof about any of this,' said Mr. Sedman with legal cautiousness. 'It's all conjecture.'

'But it fits the situation,' said Heron. 'By the way, did Sir Percival rent a safe deposit?'

'Not that I know. His bank would be

able to tell you, perhaps.'

'Wouldn't they have told you?'

'Not necessarily. I wasn't the executor, you know. The bank acted in that capacity.'

There seemed nothing more to be learned from Mr. Sedman, and Heron took his leave. From a call-office he rang up the bank. Mr. Crenate, the manager, was still there and agreed to see him, if a little reluctantly.

He was welcomed, when he arrived, with old-fashioned courtesy. Mr. Crenate was a grey-haired, thinnish man, a little punctilious and important and inclined to be uncommunicative. He had read of the murder in Bishop's Trencham and was mildly interested. He was even more interested when Heron told him of the second murder.

'So far as I know, Mr. Heron,' he said in answer to Heron's question, 'Sir Percival did not rent a safe in a safe deposit. He rented a safe with us, which, of course, was opened at the time of his death. There was nothing of importance, nothing at all.'

'I suppose you were aware of Sir Percival's fears concerning the economic situation?'

A faint smile crossed the thin face of the bank manager.

'Oh, yes,' he answered. 'He was extremely worried. I tried to reassure him but I don't think with much effect. He said it was the beginning of the end when this country went off the gold standard. His argument was that paper money had no real value. To some extent, of course, he was right. Unless backed up by collateral . . . '

Heron heard the precise voice droning on but he was only listening with half his mind. Was it possible that Sir Percival had converted his fortune into gold? And was it this gold, hidden somewhere in Trencham Close, that was at the bottom of the whole business?

10

1

Felix Heron roused himself to find Mr. Crenate watching him curiously.

'You are thinking,' he remarked with a smile, 'that Sir Percival may have converted his money into gold?'

'Would it be possible?'

Mr. Crenate screwed up his lips.

'It would be very difficult,' he said, shaking his head. 'Very difficult indeed.' He picked up a pen and rolled it gently up and down the blotting pad. 'I can say, very definitely, that gold to the amount of two hundred and twenty thousand pounds except for special reasons, could only be bought by illegal methods . . .'

'Which Sir Percival wouldn't have done?'

'Certainly not!'

'This wouldn't apply to say — diamonds?'

'Oh, no! That would present little difficulty.'

Felix Heron drove back to Park Lane in a thoughtful mood. Diamonds would fit the situation very well. Their value would remain practically static, they could be sold in any country in the world without difficulty, and they could be hidden without taking up very much space.

Heron had collected over a period of years a number of sources of information, some unsavoury, some respectable. Among these latter was a Hatton Garden diamond dealer. Mr. Saul Papiat knew most things that happened in the diamond market, and Heron put through a call to his office as soon as he reached his flat.

Mr. Papiat was in, and expressed himself as delighted to hear from his friend. He listened to what Heron had to say and promised that he would make inquiries and let him know at once if he could get the information required.

'Sometimes these deals are very secret, you understand,' he said. 'The diamond business is carried on, sometimes, with the utmost discreetness. Would this man, you mention, have bought the stones in his own name?'

'That I can't say. I should imagine so . . .'

'Leave it to me,' said Mr. Papiat. 'I will put out the inquiries, you understand? I have many contacts.'

'Wouldn't you have heard if stones for this amount had been bought?' asked Heron.

'My dear friend, the amount you mention is not such a large one in this business. It is a respectable sum, yes. But by no means outstanding, you understand?'

Heron left Mr. Papiat to conduct his inquiries and rang up Waldron. The Chief Superintendent was out. He got through to Trencham Close and spoke to Charles Rayner. He would not, he said, be able to get back until the following day — perhaps not even then. He was following a line that might explain everything and he could best attend to it in London.

He was to be recalled to Bishop's Trencham urgently, but of this he was unaware until later.

Dick Farrell passed on Felix Heron's message concerning Cripps to Thelma within a matter of half an hour after he had put down the receiver.

He found Mrs. Leyton and Marian discussing the former's marriage problems with Thelma in the sitting-room when he reached the cottage.

'Yes, I know Cripps,' said Thelma. 'Does Felix think he's down here?'

'Apparently,' said Dick.

'How's he getting on? Did he say?'

Dick shook his head.

'I've told you all he said. Now, I must be off. I'm going down to the post-office . . . '

'I'll come with you,' interrupted Thelma. 'You won't mind being left alone, you two, will you?'

'Of course not,' said Marian. 'It's a long time since I've seen Isobel . . . '

'That's right, then,' said Thelma. 'If you want to make any tea, you'll find everything you want in the kitchen. I shan't be long.'

As they left the cottage, Thelma gave a sigh of relief.

'I'm glad of an excuse to leave them to it!' she said.

'What's going to happen to that girl?' asked Dick.

'Isobel? She'll be all right. Felix will fix up something for her.'

On the way to the village they met Inspector Trafford. He looked at them with his usual unprepossessing expression of mingled suspicion and irritability.

'I hear that Mr. Heron has gone to London,' he remarked, infusing into his tone the rebuke of a school teacher admonishing a small boy. 'He shouldn't have left without informing me!'

'Why not?' asked Thelma.

'This is a murder inquiry, m'am,' said the inspector. 'Nobody concerned should've left the district without my permission.'

'Rubbish!' exclaimed Dick.

Trafford's small eyes gleamed angrily.

'I don't like your attitude, Mr. Farrell,' he snapped.

'I don't like yours!' retorted Dick.

'I'm only doing my duty, eh?'

'Or exceeding it!'

'That's not for you to say, eh? I am only responsible to my superiors.' He puffed out his red cheeks. 'It strikes me that there is a conspiracy to hamper me in my investigation, eh?'

'I'm sure we are all anxious to be helpful,' put in Thelma sweetly. 'If there's anything you would like us to do, you have only to ask!'

There was nothing to take exception to in the words, but the tone in which they were uttered was almost an insult. The inspector slowly turned purple. He opened his mouth to retort, thought better of it, and turned away.

Dick laughed as they turned into the High Street.

'What an ass that fellow is,' he said.

'A dangerous ass,' answered Thelma. 'That type of man can do a lot of damage . . .'

She broke off and caught him by the arm.

'Look!' she whispered.

Dick followed the direction of her eyes. Alfred Lessinger was standing near the entrance to Church Passage, talking to a small, shabbily dressed man with thin, sandy hair. As Dick saw him Lessinger shook his head and walked away. The little man looked after him for a moment, shrugged his shoulders, and turned in the other direction.

'Felix was right!' said Thelma.

'Right?'

'That man Alfred Lessinger was talking to — that's Cripps!'

'I'll go and grab him!' said Dick.

'No, don't!'

'Why not?'

'It might not be what Felix wants,' said Thelma. 'Follow him. See where he goes and what he does. He knows me but he doesn't know you. I don't think he saw us together. Go on — hurry!'

She gave him a gentle push and with a nod he set off in the wake of Mr. Stephen Cripps.

3

Thelma telephoned Felix Heron and told him about seeing Cripps.

'He was talking to Lessinger,' she said. 'Looks a bit fishy, doesn't it? Dick Farrell followed Cripps. He hasn't come back yet, but I'll get him to phone you himself and tell you what happened.'

'I shall be interested. At least we know definitely that Cripps is mixed up in this business . . . '

'Yes. How did you get on? Anything fresh?'

'Quite a lot. I won't tell you over the phone. I'll save it until I see you.'

'That's right — leave me with a cliff-hanger!' she said. 'When are you coming back?'

'I can't be sure. As soon as I can.'

'You'd better, or Inspector Trafford will be having you pulled in!'

'Why, what's happened?' he demanded.

'I'll save it until I see you!' retorted Thelma in a voice that dripped with honey, and rang off.

Heron grimaced, and he was just putting down the receiver when Chief Superintendent Waldron was shown in.

'Sorry I wasn't in when you phoned,' he said, taking off his hat and raincoat and throwing them on a chair. 'Anything urgent?'

'Sit down and have a drink,' said Heron.

Waldron lowered his heavy body into an easy chair.

'Don't mind if I do,' he grunted.

'Whisky, isn't it?'

Waldron nodded. Heron went over to the cocktail cabinet and took out a bottle of John Haig.

'Say when,' he invited.

'Make it a good stiff one, if you don't mind,' said Waldron. 'Without water or soda. Both spoil a good whisky in my opinion.'

Heron poured out a generous portion and took it over. Waldron gulped half of it and grunted with appreciation.

'Good stuff!' he said. ''Fraid I've no news for you. Can't find that little beggar, Cripps, anywhere . . . '

'Don't worry,' said Heron. 'I've found him!'

'Have you, by George! Where?'

'He's in Bishop's Trencham.'

'How do you know?'

'Thelma rang up just before you arrived. She saw him.'

'I wonder what he's doing there?' muttered Waldron.

'The same business as Mellins, I expect,' said Heron. 'Let's hope that it turns out better for him than it did for his pal.'

Waldron finished his whisky.

'From what you've told me,' he said, 'this seems a pretty queer affair. It's not our business, of course. We haven't been asked to help — except to identify that print belonging to the dead man.'

'Oh, Trafford sent the prints, did he?' Heron took the empty glass and refilled it from the John Haig bottle without asking.

'By special messenger!' said the Chief Superintendent accepting the fresh drink with a nod of thanks. 'I asked F.P. to let me have the result.'

'If any!' remarked Heron.

'Oh, there was a result all right! They spotted the feller almost at once. Chap called Michael Drebner. He had a string of aliases but that was his real name. Been inside several times. Spent nearly a third of his life inside.'

'And that's the chap who was killed?'

'It is — if those were his prints.' Waldron took a sip of his whisky. 'Like to put me in the picture? All I know at the moment is a bit scrappy. Fill me in.'

'Right you are!' Heron sat down and told the interested superintendent all about it. When he had finished, Waldron rubbed his chin with a large hand.

'Complicated business,' he commented. 'It's all yours. I should say you'd got the right end of it. Two hundred and twenty thousands pounds worth of diamonds is enough to attract all the crooks in London.'

'It's all conjecture. There's no proof that there are any diamonds.'

'Shouldn't be difficult to trace a lot like that,' said Waldron. 'Unless, of course, they were 'hot' . . . '

'Trench wouldn't have touched anything like that . . . '

'Not if he knew. Have you thought of that? Lot of smuggled stuff and I.D.B. always changing hands, you know.'

'Yes, there's always that possibility,' agreed Heron.

'Difficult to trace, eh? These people

don't advertise their deals. I know one or two of 'em. I'll have a nose round . . . '

'I wish you would . . . '

At that moment the telephone bell rang.

'Excuse me,' said Heron, getting up and going over to the instrument. 'This may be Farrell with news of Cripps . . . '

But it was Thelma! Her voice sounded faint and he had difficulty in hearing what she said.

'Is that you Felix? Listen, can you come back at once, darling.'

'What's happened?' he asked sharply. 'I can't hear you very well, dear — bad line.'

'It's Dick Farrell.' Her voice was still faint. 'He's disappeared!'

'Disappeared?'

'He hasn't come back since he left me to follow Cripps.' Quite suddenly his wife's voice came over clear and strong. 'I'm afraid it's serious. A constable found his hat near Denham Wood. It was covered with blood!'

'I'll come down straight away,' said Heron. 'By car. Don't do anything until I get there. 'Bye!'

He slammed down the receiver and pressed the bell for Harry.

'I want the car — at once, Harry!' he said curtly when the secretary arrived. 'I'm going to Bishop's Trencham.'

'What's the matter?' asked Waldron.

'Farrell's disappeared and his hat has been found all over blood!' said Heron. 'He was following Cripps . . . '

'You're going down now?'

'Yes, at once . . . '

'Can I come with you? I'm off duty tomorrow . . . '

'There's nothing I should like better,' declared Heron. 'Come on, let's go!'

11

1

Dick Farrell lit a cigarette and followed the thin, shuffling figure of Mr. Cripps. The little man, after leaving Alfred Lessinger, had moved off down the village High Street. He walked with his head down so that his chin almost touched his narrow chest. Once he glanced quickly round and darted a sharp glance at Dick. But if he was suspicious he gave no outward sign but continued on his way.

They came to the end of the High Street and Cripps crossed the road towards the one and only pub which the village boasted. It was just opening time and Mr. Cripps entered the public bar.

Dick followed casually, taking no notice of the other. Mr. Cripps gave him a suspicious glance but Dick went straight up to the counter and ordered a pint of bitter. The landlord served him first, and then turned his attention to Mr. Cripps.

'Pint o' mild,' said the little man.

The landlord drew the beer, took the money and retired to the back of the bar and a newspaper that he was reading. Out of the corner of his eye Dick watched Mr. Cripps take a pull at his beer and wipe his lips with the back of his hand. He took out a packet of cheap cigarettes, lit one, inhaling the smoke and letting it dribble out of his nostrils.

Dick took stock of him more closely. His appearance was not at all prepossessing. His complexion was unhealthy. It was not pale but a dirty grey. His eyes were small, weak, and shifty and his chin was almost non-existent. His lips were loose and wet, and his shabby overcoat, once blue, was now so stained and faded that little of the original colour remained. His sandy hair was dirty and hung over his low forehead in rat's tails. He looked rather like a starving weasel.

'Know of any lodgin's rahn 'ere?' asked Mr. Cripps in a cockney whine, addressing the landlord.

'Don't know as I do,' answered the

landlord. 'It ain't often we gets anyone lookin' fer lodgin's. Let me see, now. I did 'ear as Mrs. Dollop was wantin' ter let a room now that 'er son's got a job in Lunnon.'

'Where does she 'ang out?' asked Mr. Cripps.

'Go along ter the end of this street,' said the landlord. 'There be a bit of a lane that runs off to the right. Don't take no notice of that, go on until yer comes to the next lane on the same side. You'll come to a stile that gives on to a footpath. It crosses a medder. Go along that until yer come to another stile. It brings yer out on a narrer road. If yer turn to the left you'll see three cottages. Mrs. Dollop lives in the middle one. Tell 'er Sam Parkins sent yer. That's me. She'll know.'

Mr. Cripps grunted which may have been his way of expressing his thanks, and ordered another pint of mild.

So, thought Dick, the man was considering staying in the village. He determined to find out why and not to let Mr. Cripps out of his sight. The man was consuming his second pint more slowly, and Dick ordered another bitter for himself. When it was brought he moved nearer to the little man.

'Good drop of beer,' he said cheerfully.

The small eyes regarded him coldly.

'I've drunk better an' I've drunk worse,' said Mr. Cripps non-committally.

'I've drunk worse but certainly not better,' said Dick good-humouredly. 'Home brewed, landlord?'

The landlord shook his bald head.

'There ain't much 'ome brewed these days, sir,' he said. 'Not round these parts. That beer comes from Binks Brewery. Nice drop o' stuff. But o' course a lot depends on the way yer keeps it. You're stayin' up at the Close, ain't yer, sir?'

Dick could have slain the landlord on the spot. The man had given him away in all innocence, but he could see by the change in Mr. Cripps's expression that the damage was done.

'Queer lot o' things goin' on up at the Close, from all accounts,' continued the landlord happily. 'Someone was shot, so I 'ear, last night.'

The suspicion in Mr. Cripps's small

167

eyes deepened. He was looking at Dick with open hostility. Blissfully unconscious of the consternation he was causing the landlord went cheerfully on:

'There's bin a lot o' rumours flyin' around, sir. They do say that Sir Percival's death weren't no accident.'

'It's better not to believe all you hear,' said Dick.

'All the same, sir,' continued the landlord, producing as it were his trump card from up his sleeve, 'this 'ere detective chap from Lunnon wouldn't be 'ere if there weren't somethin' in it.'

Dick made an evasive reply. The mischief was done! Mr. Cripps would be on his guard. The situation would have to be handled with extreme care. Confound the landlord! Dick had no idea that he would be recognized when he followed the little man into the pub, although he ought to have been prepared. In a village as small as this, gossip circulates with almost the speed of light, and strangers are regarded with intense interest and curiosity. It was no good staying — not now. It would be better to go before Mr.

Cripps and think up some other method of keeping him under his eyes than by following him.

He emptied his glass, nodded to the landlord, and left the bar. Walking along the little High Street he considered his next move.

It would be stupid to hang about in the vicinity of the pub for Mr. Cripps to come out. If the little man spotted him it would be all up with any chance of following him. The best thing to do would be to make his way to Mrs. Dollop's cottage and watch for Mr. Cripps's arrival. This involved a certain amount of risk. He might lose the man altogether, or Mr. Cripps might go somewhere else first.

However, it seemed the better bet in the circumstances. Dick set off to find his way to Mrs. Dollop's. He remembered the landlord's directions and followed them. Reaching the end of the High Street he found the little lane. It took a winding course between high hedges, and presently he came to the stile. A footpath straggled across a meadow and this led to the second stile. Beyond was a road lined on either side by strips of grass.

Dick walked along until he found the three cottages. They were set back from the road, behind little gardens, and faced a wide expanse of pastureland. Dick slowed down as he passed the cottages and took a hasty look round for possible cover.

The road took a wide bend to the left and in the elbow thus formed was a tumbledown building that looked like a barn. It did not seem to have any connection with the cottages but stood in a corner of a fenced-in field. A short distance farther along there was a gate that led into the field. The barn was just the thing he was looking for. It was very dilapidated and appeared to be unused. From it he could keep an eye on the movements of Mr. Cripps — if he came!

The road was empty, and quickly he climbed over the gate. A few steps brought him to the barn and he saw that the crazy door was hanging half-off its hinges. He squeezed through into the dark and musty-smelling interior. He soon found a knothole in the rotten wood from which he could see the row of cottages, and, pulling up an old packing-case he sat down.

He had no idea how long he might have to wait and decided that he might as well be as comfortable as possible. It was over an hour later before Mr. Cripps put in an appearance.

He paused at the gate of Mrs. Dollop's cottage, hesitated a second, and then shuffled up the little garden path to the front door. He knocked and waited. After a few seconds the door was opened. Evidently Mrs. Dollop decided to let her son's room, for Mr. Cripps went in and the door was shut.

So far so good! What would be the next move from the little man? Would he remain in for the night, or would he sally forth to transact whatever nefarious business had brought him to the village? The only thing to do was wait!

The time dragged slowly by and there was no sign of the reappearance of Mr. Cripps. It looked as if he had dug himself in for the night!

Dick was beginning to feel hungry. The purple dusk of the evening was settling down over the country and it was nearly dark. Lights were showing in the windows of the three cottages and still there was no Cripps!

Dick eased himself into a more comfortable position. He would have liked to smoke but he hadn't any cigarettes. But he dare not leave! Even if it meant an all-night vigil he would have to stay. There was no telling when Mr. Cripps might decide to make a move. But it was not a pleasant prospect!

Suddenly he heard the click of a latch and a dim ray of light fanned out from Mrs. Dollop's front door! It shone for barely a second and then was blotted out as the door was shut. But in the moment when it illuminated the little path, Dick had seen the thin figure of Mr. Cripps issue forth!

Dick could scarcely see the dim figure that shuffled down the path to the gate, but when he reached the gate someone in an upstairs room of the adjoining cottage pulled aside the curtain and the light from the window picked out the little man clearly.

He opened the garden gate, looked up and down the road, and then set off in the direction from which he had come.

Dick blessed the curiosity of the person who had looked to see who was leaving Mrs. Dollop's. He slipped quickly out of the old barn, over the gate, and began to follow Mr. Cripps, keeping to the grass verge to deaden his footsteps.

It was quite dark by now and he found it difficult to see the man he was following. It was an advantage in a way because if he could not see Mr. Cripps, Mr. Cripps could not see him! He could hear the other's uneven steps and these served as something of a guide.

He expected that Cripps would climb over the stile to the footpath across the meadow, but he continued on along the road. Where was he making for? The road took a sharp curve and Dick guessed that it led to the village — a longer way round than the short cut over the stile.

The road began to narrow and the hedges gave way to gaunt trees that became thicker until one side of the road passed by the fringe of a wood.

And quite suddenly the footsteps ahead stopped!

Dick pulled up and held his breath. Mr. Cripps had either halted or taken to the grass on the side of the road. Which?

There came to his straining ears the scrape of a match. In the little flicker of the flame he saw that Mr. Cripps was standing by a finger of stone that projected from the edge of the ditch.

The match was extinguished almost at once but its place was taken by the glow from a cigarette. Dick watched the red spark and saw that Mr. Cripps was making no move to continue his journey. He had stopped by the side of the milestone and was waiting — for what?

Obviously an appointment with some-one, thought Dick. The road was lonely and the milestone offered an excellent landmark An ideal spot for a secret meeting.

Dick felt a little thrill of excitement. At least he was going to be rewarded for his long and uncomfortable vigil. Ten minutes passed. Mr. Cripps finished his cigarette and threw away the stub which hit the grass with a little shower of sparks. There was another interval of silence and then the sound of footsteps came faintly to Dick's ears. Somebody was approaching rapidly from the direction of the village. Louder and more distinct they came, crunching on the rough surface of the road. They stopped and there was the murmur of voices.

Dick could see nothing of the newcomer, neither could he distinguish what was being said. It was essential that he should know who had come to meet Mr. Cripps and to hear what they were saying.

Tingling with excitement, he crept forward. As he drew nearer, the voices became more distinct. He was able to pick up a word here and there . . .

'Mellins tried the same game . . . '

The voice was gruff, certainly it was not Mr. Cripps who was speaking.

' . . . such a fool. I ain't come 'ere without . . . ' This was definitely the voice of Mr. Cripps. In his eagerness to hear more, Dick took a step forward — and trod on a dead branch!

It snapped with a report like a pistol

shot! He heard a startled oath, followed by a rush of feet. A dark form sprang at him out of the blackness. He turned to defend himself. But he was too late!

Something hit him on the head and at the same time there was an explosion close to his ear, and a flash of flame seared his cheek. Pain swamped his senses and he knew nothing more . . .

2

There were lights in the windows of Trencham Close when Felix Heron and Chief Superintendent Waldron arrived. The first person to greet them was Thelma.

'We've found Dick Farrell,' she said. 'He's in a pretty bad condition, though . . .'

'What happened? Where did you find him?' asked Heron.

'Come into the drawing-room,' said Thelma, 'and I'll tell you all about it. Good evening, Superintendent, though I suppose it should really be 'good morning.''

'How are you, Mrs. Heron,' said

Waldron, taking off his overcoat and depositing it on a carved oak chest. 'You've had an exciting time, apparently.'

'I thrive on excitement!' she answered. 'Come along. The servants are in bed but the rest of us are up.'

Heron left his overcoat on the top of Waldron's, and they followed her into the drawing-room. Rayner was standing in front of the fire, and Harry Glenn was sprawled in an easy chair. Marian, they learned later, was staying up at the cottage with Isobel Leyton.

'Glad you're back,' said Rayner. 'I expect you'd like a drink after your journey?'

'I'd like a very large pink gin,' said Heron. He introduced Waldron, and Rayner shook hands.

'Glad to have you with us,' he said. 'What can I get you?'

Waldron chose whisky, and Rayner went away to get the drinks.

'Now,' said Heron, 'tell us what happened.'

'After they found his hat,' said Thelma, 'and it was reported to Trafford, a search

177

was made. We all joined in . . . '

'I found him,' put in Harry Glenn. 'He was lying in some undergrowth just inside Denham Wood. He was unconscious and there was a wound on his temple. There were powder marks all over his forehead. Apparently, he'd been shot at close range. There was also a large swelling on the back of his head . . . '

'He'd been coshed as well as shot,' said Thelma, taking up the story. 'He was taken to the Cottage Hospital. Luckily, the bullet only ploughed the side of his head but he's still unconscious. They've promised to ring through when he recovers.'

'You left him following Cripps?' asked Heron and she nodded. 'I wonder what happened between then and the time he was found? It was quite a while.'

'He'll be able to tell us when he comes to his senses,' said Glenn. 'I thought he was a goner when I found him.'

Rayner came in with a tray containing glasses, a bottle of Gordon's gin, angostura, and whisky. He set this down on a side table and began to mix the drinks.

'Here you are, Superintendent,' he said,

pouring out a large John Haig, and bringing it over to Waldron. 'What will you have with it, soda or water?'

'I'll have it neat, thank you,' said Waldron. 'I doubt if Cripps was entirely responsible for this,' he went on. 'He never carried a gun. Too scared . . . '

Rayner gave Heron his pink gin.

'Why should he have been attacked at all?' he asked.

Heron shrugged his shoulders.

'Obviously he stumbled on something that was dangerous to someone . . . '

'The chap who killed Drebner?' put in Waldron. 'I think that's more likely . . . '

'Who's Drebner?' asked Rayner.

'He's the man who was shot in the rose garden,' answered Heron. He explained briefly what they had found out from the dead man's prints.

'I've been wondering,' said Thelma, 'whether Alfred Lessinger could be at the bottom of all this. He was talking to Cripps when we spotted him, you know.'

'Could be, of course,' said Heron. 'We don't know enough to form an opinion. I'd like to have a look at the place where you found Farrell, Glenn, when it gets light.' He yawned. 'Meanwhile, we'd all better get some sleep. I've an idea that we're going to be in for a pretty strenuous time shortly.'

How right he was they were soon to discover.

12

1

The morning dawned bright, clear and frosty. Rayner had insisted on putting Chief Superintendent Waldron up at Trencham Close but Heron and Thelma had elected to drive up to the cottage.

In spite of the small amount of sleep he had had, Felix Heron was up early. Marian and Isobel Leyton were both fast asleep when he and Thelma sat down to a hasty breakfast of toast and coffee.

Heron had arranged, before leaving Trencham Close, that he would call and pick up Harry Glenn at seven o'clock, and at a quarter to that hour he set off, leaving Thelma at the cottage.

Glenn was ready and waiting when he arrived and together they went to the place in Denham Wood where Harry had found his friend.

The undergrowth was trodden down by

the feet of the men who had come to take the wounded man away and there was no possibility of finding any traces of the people responsible for the attack on Dick Farrell.

'Where did they find the hat?' asked Heron. 'Do you know?'

Glenn not only knew but took him to the spot.

Heron surveyed the ground in disappointment.

'Looks as if a herd of cattle had been here!' he grunted. 'I suppose this mess was made by Trafford and his men?'

Glenn nodded.

'I expect it will be a waste of time but we may as well look,' said Heron.

'What for?' asked Harry.

'I'll show you if I find it!' said Heron.

He began to search about, examining the ground that had been stamped almost flat by the passing of many feet. It seemed almost impossible to find any separate footprint among that jumble but Felix Heron persevered. And his diligence was rewarded. A short distance away, close in against a strip of grass he found one clear print.

But it was enough!

Clear in the mud was the print of a broad-toed shoe — the same print that had left its marks in the dust of the disused cottage and had been imprinted in the wet gravel near the wall in the rose garden at Trencham Close. The footprint of the man who had shot Michael Drebner!

'That clinches it!' said Heron, pointing it out to Glenn. 'It was the same man who killed Drebner who was mixed up with wounding Farrell.'

'But we're no nearer finding out who it belongs to,' said Glenn.

They went back to Trencham Close. The household was up, and Charles Rayner and Waldron were having breakfast. The chief superintendent was a little annoyed.

'You might have let me come with you,' he grumbled when he learned where they had been at such an early hour.

'Do you more good to sleep!' said Heron. 'Has there been any message from the hospital?'

Rayner shook his head.

'That means that Farrell is still un-conscious,' remarked Heron. He accepted Rayner's offer of coffee. 'You know, I'm wondering why he got off so lightly. These people might have finished the job . . . '

'Perhaps they thought they had?' suggested Waldron. 'That wound in the head must be quite serious or Farrell would have recovered before now . . . '

Stukes came in to announce that Inspector Trafford wished to see them. Before they could say anything, Trafford followed him into the dining-room. His small eyes narrowed when he saw Heron.

'So you've come back, eh?' he grunted. 'You'd no right to leave without my permission . . . '

'I apologise!' said Heron meekly. 'Let me introduce you to Detective Chief Superintendent Waldron, C.I.D. New Scotland Yard.'

Trafford was taken aback. He frowned. His displeasure was obvious.

'I have not asked for any assistance,' he said.

'I'm not here in an official capacity,' broke in Waldron genially. 'I came down as a friend of Mr. Heron's, that's all.'

'I see,' said Trafford ungraciously. 'So long as it is clearly understood that I don't want any interference . . . '

Waldron reddened with annoyance.

'Nobody is going to interfere with you,' he said, swallowing his anger with an effort. 'But I'm sure that you will welcome any assistance that we are able to offer.'

'My own men can give me all the assistance that I need!' said the inspector stiffly. 'I should much prefer to be left to conduct this business in my own way!'

'It would be interesting to hear what the chief constable would say about your refusal to accept experienced assistance, offered in a friendly and unofficial capacity!' remarked Heron.

The expression of Trafford's face changed. There was a trace of uneasiness in his pig-like eyes as he said:

'Of course, if you know anything that would help to clear this matter up,' he said, 'it's your duty to tell me. But I want facts, not theories!'

'Exactly! Chief Superintendent Waldron has brought you evidence of the identity of the man who was shot in the rose garden!'

'Is that so, eh? That'll be a great help.'

Waldron took the envelope containing a photograph and record of Michael Drebner from his pocket and pushed it across the table to Heron who picked it up and handed it to Trafford. The inspector took it and opened it. He peered at the contents and his low forehead corrugated in a frown. Before he could make any comment, however, Stukes came in again.

'Excuse me, sir,' said the butler to Rayner. 'Mr. Lessinger has called. He would like to see you, sir, at once.'

'Ask him to come in,' said Rayner promptly. He looked at Heron. 'What does *he* want, I wonder?'

'I expect he'll tell us!' murmured Heron.

Alfred Lessinger was ushered in a few seconds later, and came, hesitantly, and not a little nervously.

'Good m-morning,' he said. 'I'm v-very sorry to disturb you so early, but my sister thinks that I s-should acquaint you with rather an extraordinary incident . . . '

'Sit down, Mr. Lessinger,' said Rayner. 'Please don't apologise. We're getting used to extraordinary incidents here. No doubt you've heard of our latest trouble?'

Lessinger blinked at him through his spectacles and slowly shook his head.

'N-no, I'm afraid I d-don't know what you mean. I've heard n-nothing.'

Heron told him about the attack on Dick Farrell, and his long face grew even longer in his astonishment, and concern.

'Good gracious! Really, this is getting t-terrible! What can be the reason for all this violence? One will b-be afraid to g-go out after d-dark soon . . . '

'What was this incident you came to tell us about?' broke in Heron.

'Ah, yes. Well, it was most extraordinary — m-most extraordinary. It m-may well be helpful. I don't know. It occurred in the High Street. I had been to inquire if some books I had ordered had arrived at the r-railway station. They had n-not. On m-my way back I was a-accosted by this m-man.' He paused and cleared his throat. Heron glanced at Waldron. Had Lessinger decided on this visit to forestall any inquiries that might be made concerning his meeting with Stephen Cripps? Was he offering an explanation before he could be questioned?

'He was a s-small man, thin with s-sandy hair,' Alfred Lessinger went on. 'I thought he was g-going to ask m-me the way s-somewhere, but he addressed me as if he knew me! 'Hello, Drebner,' he said, 'How's it going?' I was too a-astonished to answer, and he went on: 'Didn't expect to see me, eh? Well, I'm always out for a bit of easy money, so what about it?' I told him that I d-din't know w-what he was t-talking about. 'Don't try that stuff on me, mate,' he said. 'It won't work with Steve Cripps.' I again a-assured him that he was m-mistaken, but he got q-quite abusive. 'I'll get tough if you don't play ball,' he said, and his manner was most threatening. And then he s-suddenly c-calmed down. 'I'm sorry, guv'nor,' he said. 'I made a mistake. I thought you was a friend o' mine, but I see you ain't.' He shuffled off. It was e-evident that he'd m-made a mistake. He must have thought I w-was that chap who w-was killed.'

He looked round, peering at them short-sightedly.

'I forgot all a-about the incident, but when I remembered it and m-mentioned it t-to my s-sister she told m-me I ought t-to tell you a-about it.'

There was a short silence. If Lessinger had thought up this story it was a very plausible one — so plausible that it might be the truth.

'Thank you, Mr. Lessinger,' said Heron. 'It was good of you to take so much trouble to come here and tell us. We are already aware of the identity of the man who was killed. His name was Michael Drebner, so Cripps could easily have made a mistake.'

'Who's this Cripps, eh?' demanded Trafford who had listened in frowning silence.

'He is, or was, a friend of the man who was hanged on that tree,' said Heron. 'My wife saw him talking to Mr. Lessinger and suggested to Mr. Farrell that he should follow Cripps . . . '

'This is the first I've heard of it,' grunted Trafford. 'Why wasn't I told, eh?'

'There's been no time . . . '

'Time should have been made. This is important, eh? This man Cripps was responsible for the attack on Mr. Farrell, eh?'

'I think it was the other man who was mostly responsible for that.'

'What other man?'

'The man who shot Drebner. I found his footprint at the place where Mr. Farrell's hat was found. It was the same print as the one on the rose garden.'

'There are too many people messing about in this case,' grumbled Trafford. 'I don't like the way things are being kept from me . . . '

'If you don't like it, inspector,' snapped Felix Heron, his patience exhausted, 'you had better make a complaint to the right quarter! No doubt it will be treated with the attention it deserves!'

A flush spread slowly over Trafford's thick neck and heavy face. He opened his mouth to reply, thought better of it, and remained silent. Alfred Lessinger rose to his feet.

'I'll b-be getting b-back home,' he said.

He wished them all good morning and Heron went with him to the door.

'Tell your sister that I hope to be seeing her later today,' he said opening the front door. 'It was good of you to come over specially.'

'N-not at all,' said Lessinger.

Heron watched the rather ungainly, stooping figure as it went down the drive. Had Lessinger been speaking the truth? It was difficult to be sure.

He was turning back to re-enter the house when he caught sight of something on the wet gravel of the drive close to the steps leading up to the porch. Hurrying down the steps he looked closer. He had not been mistaken! There, near the bottom step, was a footprint, sharp and clearly marked.

It was the broad-toed footprint of Michael Drebner's murderer!

2

Felix Heron said nothing of his discovery when he rejoined the others in the dining-room. But it made him very thoughtful. It had certainly not been made by Lessinger. He had taken particular note of the stout boots which he had been wearing. They were smaller and of a totally different shape to those that had made the print on the gravel. But the finding of the print where it was proved that the murderer had recently been in the vicinity of the house. The print had partially obliterated one of his own. It couldn't have been so very long, therefore, since it had been made.

Inspector Trafford took his departure a few minutes later, an angry and disgruntled man, and soon after he had gone, Rayner telephoned the hospital to inquire how Dick Farrell was. The matron reported that there was no change.

'It looks bad to me,' said Glenn. 'Do you think we ought to get another doctor's opinion?'

Heron nodded.

'I certainly think it would do no harm,' he said. 'There should at least be an X-ray taken and I don't suppose they have facilities for that . . . '

'I'll ring the *Messenger*,' said Glenn. 'They'll get the best advice possible and attend to everything.'

'Good idea!' said Heron.

He took Waldron out to the rose garden and showed him the scene of the murder. It looked very different in the pale sunlight than in the darkness and mist of the night when Drebner had been shot. Only the stain on the stone by the sundial showed dark and sinister to mark the place where he had fallen.

'I want to talk to you,' said Heron as they strolled round the enclosed garden. 'I've an idea that might give us what we want . . .'

In a low voice he proceeded to explain. Waldron was interested.

'It might work,' he said. 'You'll have to be careful, though. If the person you want gets an inkling that it's a put up job, it'll go for a burton.'

'You can come with me and we'll pick up Thelma on the way,' said Heron. 'We ought to be back by lunch time.'

They were back in plenty of time. Charles Rayner was drinking a Dry Fly sherry when they came in. He didn't inquire where they had been, concluding that it must have been to pick up Thelma whom they had brought back with them. He gave Thelma a sherry and mixed a Gordon's pink gin for Heron. Waldron chose a sherry. They learned that Harry Glenn had gone down to the hospital and had not come back yet.

'I believe Dick's newspaper is sending down a specialist,' said Rayner. 'Glenn's gone to make arrangement's with the doctor at the hospital. I've offered to put him up here.'

'I'm glad,' said Thelma, sipping her Dry Fly. 'I shall feel much happier to know that Dick's getting the best attention.'

'So shall I,' said Rayner. 'I feel responsible, in a way. He came down here at my invitation.' He shook his head. 'I wish I'd never bought this place!' he said.

'It's a very lovely property,' said Heron. 'When all this is over you'll be able to enjoy it in peace . . . '

'When will it be over?' demanded Rayner. 'Something else keeps on happening. By the way, when is Marian coming back?'

'She doesn't want to leave her friend on her own,' said Thelma. 'I can't be there all the time, you see . . . '

Rayner frowned.

'I don't like her getting mixed up with Mrs. Leyton,' he said.

'I can assure you that Isobel Leyton is a very nice girl,' said Thelma. 'She got married to a really nasty bit of work who took every penny she had and knocked her about into the bargain. She stuck it out as long as she could, longer than I would have done, and in my opinion she was quite right to leave him . . . '

Whether Rayner would have put up an argument they never knew because the arrival of Stukes to announce that luncheon was served, coinciding with the return of Harry Glenn, stopped all further discussion of the subject.

'The local doctor and the hospital are very pleased to have a specialist's opinion,' said Glenn, as they sat down to the meal. 'In my estimation they are very relieved to share the responsibility.'

'Did you see Dick?' asked Rayner.

'Yes. I don't like the look of him at all.

I think his condition is serious.'

'When is this specialist arriving?' asked Heron.

'Early this afternoon, according to what they told me at the *Messenger*.'

They were having coffee and brandy in the drawing-room when Heron put up the suggestion that was to have such far-reaching results.

'You know,' he remarked sipping his Hennessy, 'I don't think we've exhausted the possibility that that book is in this house.'

'But we searched everywhere,' expostulated Rayner.

'Agreed! But did we do it thoroughly?'

'We had every book down off the shelves,' said Glenn. 'I don't know what more we can do . . . '

'We didn't look *inside* every book,' said Heron.

'What's the point?'

'If you wanted to conceal a book among a lot of other books what would you do?'

'I'll buy it,' said Glenn. 'What?'

'Wouldn't it be a good idea to put your

book *inside* the binding of one of the others? I mean substitute the contents but leave the *outside* the same . . . '

'I've got you! Take the binding off this book and replace it with another?'

'Yes, and that's what I believe Sir Percival did.'

'Let's go through those books again, then. That'll prove whether you're right or not!' said Glenn.

They went into the library and the five of them set to work. It was a long job. They were all weary when Rayner made the discovery.

'Here you are,' he called excitedly. 'I've found it! You were right, Heron! Look!'

They came over to him. He was holding a red-covered volume labelled *Pope's Essays*. The original fly-leaf was attached, but except for that there was nothing of the work of Mr. Pope remaining.

The rest of the book consisted of Edgar Wallace's *The Sinister Man*!

13

1

The book was disappointing. It was a new edition and the cover of *Pope's Essays* had been fastened over the original cover with strips of Selotape.

But there was nothing to distinguish it from any other edition of the same book. There was no mark on any of the pages, no words underlined, no writing, no message of any kind that they could discover.

'Well, that's the book,' said Felix Heron. 'But, so far as I can see, it doesn't contain anything at all except the original story.'

'Why take so much trouble to conceal it?' said Glenn.

'There must be something,' declared Rayner.

'Undoubtedly there is. But what?'

'Perhaps, it contains a cipher,' suggested

Rayner, frowning. 'Certain words on certain pages that compared with a list that is in the possession of these people make a message.'

'That could be,' agreed Heron. 'If so the book is useless without this list.'

'What do we do now?' asked Thelma.

Heron tucked the book under his arm.

'Keep it very carefully,' he said. 'It may reveal its secret later. I think we ought to inform Trafford that we've found it and also the Lessingers . . . '

'Do you think that's wise? Telling the Lessingers, I mean?' said Waldron.

'I don't see that it can do any harm . . . '

'Alfred Lessinger may be in this. We don't know, do we?'

Heron patted the book under his arm.

'Don't worry,' he said. 'I'll take care of this.'

Thelma shrugged her shoulders.

'I suppose you know what you're doing,' she said. 'But I should have thought that the finding of the book ought to be kept as secret as possible . . . '

Waldron nodded.

'I should have thought so, too,' he agreed.

Heron smiled at them blandly.

'That shows how little you know about it,' he said.

The telephone bell rang and Rayner picked up the receiver.

'Hello,' he said. 'Yes. Hold on a minute, will you?' He turned to Heron. 'It's for you.'

The voice of Saul Papiat came over the wire as Heron put the receiver to his ear.

'It is you, my friend? That is good. I have been busy for you, you understand? I am as you would say 'the go-getter,' eh?'

'You've found out something?'

'I make the inquiries, yes. The information that you have asked of me I have.'

'About Sir Percival?'

'Indeed, yes, my friend. You were so right. The man you are interested in bought some stones from Jacobs . . . '

'Diamonds?'

'Would I be talking of pebbles? Diamonds, my friend, of gem quality! That is what you seek, eh?'

'You've done wonders! Who is Jacobs?'

'He is a dealer, you understand? Not one of the big dealers. A small man . . . '

'Where do I find him?'

'He rents an office, not actually in Hatton Garden, you understand? I will give you the address . . . '

'Just a minute,' broke in Heron. He pulled a piece of paper from the desk on which the telephone stood and took a pencil from his pocket. 'All right, go ahead.'

He wrote down the address of Jacobs's office as Papiat gave it over the phone.

'I don't know how to thank you, Papiat,' he said. 'You've helped a lot.'

'Don't try, my friend,' said Saul Papiat. 'I help my friends when I can, you understand? You helped me once. I wish you good luck, and my regards to your so charming wife.'

Heron laid down the receiver and turned to the other three.

'That was Saul Papiat,' he said. 'You remember him, dear?'

'An old pet!' she said. 'He's found out about the diamonds?'

'Trench *did* invest that money in

201

diamonds, then?' broke in Rayner. 'You were right?'

'And they're hidden somewhere here!' said Glenn.

'I don't know about that,' said Heron. 'But Sir Percival certainly *did* buy some stones from a man called Jacobs. What he did with them we have yet to find out.'

'I'll bet the secret of that is in that book,' said Glenn. 'Though what it can be beats me.'

'Perhaps we shall find out,' said Heron. 'I'm going up to London to see this man Jacobs. You can come with me, darling, and we'll take Mrs. Leyton with us. If I drive you over to the cottage, Glenn, perhaps you'd bring Miss Rayner home?'

Harry agreed with alacrity.

'You'll come with us, won't you, Waldron?' asked Heron and the chief superintendent nodded.

'Save me having to go back by train,' he said.

A few seconds later they were in Heron's car on the way to the cottage, and the book went with them.

The office of Mr. Lewis Jacobs was on the top floor of a narrow, grimy-looking building in a mean street off Hatton Garden. Mr. Jacobs was a fat, prosperous-looking man with a fringe of black, curly hair round a bald head.

Mr. Jacobs obviously did not believe in wasting money on his surroundings, for the office in which he sat behind a large flat-topped desk was shabby and ill-furnished. The most expensive article in it consisted of a very big safe that stood against one wall on a thick concrete slab.

Mr. Jacobs looked at the card which Heron had sent in to him by a peaky, thin girl who occupied a kind of cupboard, it was little bigger, through which one had to pass before reaching the proprietor, and from the card to the man whose name it bore.

'What,' inquired Mr. Jacobs in a slightly guttural voice, and the trace of a lisp, 'can I do for you, thir?'

'I believe that you transacted some

business with the late Sir Percival Trench,' said Heron.

'I'm afraid I cannot discuss anything concerning my clients, Mr. Heron . . . '

'This is a very special inquiry,' said Heron. 'I am not asking out of idle curiosity. If you will listen to what I have to tell you, I am sure that you will do all you can to assist in the matter.'

This deliberately pompous speech appeared to impress Mr. Jacobs. He leaned back in his office chair and rested his chubby hands on the desk in front of him.

'I can't promise you that, thir,' he said. 'But I am prepared to listen to anything you have to say.'

Felix Heron told him the whole story. Mr. Jacob's large, liquid brown eyes grew larger as he proceeded.

'I understand the situation,' he said when Heron had finished. 'I will certainly do all I can. Thir Percival Trench did buy some diamonds from me — very fine stones, they were. He bought two hundred and twenty thousand pounds worth . . . '

'For which he paid in cash?'

Mr. Jacobs nodded.

'Yes. I was rather surprised, but he pointed out that he wished the fact that he had bought those stones to be secret. A cheque would have been traceable.'

'How many of these diamonds did he purchase?'

'Ten stones of gem quality. Fine blue-whites.'

'Why did he come to you, Mr. Jacobs?' asked Heron. 'Was he recommended by anyone?'

'Yes. General Akeman. They were both members of the same club. General Akeman had bought some stones from me to have set in a piece of jewellery for his daughter.'

'Did Sir Percival say *why* he wanted these diamonds?'

'He mentioned that they would be an insurance against the danger of any serious inflation. Of course, he was right! Diamonds fluctuate very little in value.'

'Now, would it have been possible for anyone to become aware of this transaction?' asked Heron.

'Not from me, thir!' Mr. Jacobs was indignant.

'No, no! I wasn't thinking of you. But you have a girl working for you. She might have overheard . . . '

'She wasn't here then. I had a clerk at the time.'

'Oh, what was his name?'

'Wyseman — James Wyseman.'

'*He* could have overheard?'

'I suppose he could, but only if he'd listened at the door . . . '

'When did he leave your employ?'

'Very soon after the deal with Sir Percival.'

'Do you know where he is to be found?'

Mr. Jacobs shook his head.

'No, I'm afraid I don't. I can give you his address when he worked here. He may still be living there.'

He drew a sheet of paper towards him and scribbled it down.

'There you are, Mr. Heron,' he said.

'Thank you very much indeed for being so helpful,' said Heron.

He took his leave of Mr. Jacobs and drove back to his flat. Thelma was talking to Isobel Leyton when he came into the lounge.

'Well, we're getting along,' he said when he had told them the result of his interview with Mr. Jacobs. 'The diamonds *are* at the bottom of this business . . . '

'All we want now,' said Thelma, 'is the identity of the murderer, and the whereabouts of the diamonds. A mere nothing!'

'I don't think the identity of the murderer is going to be difficult,' said Heron.

Thelma stared at him.

'Felix! Do you mean you know?'

'Not definitely, but I have a very good idea.'

'Who is it?'

He laughed.

'I'll tell you when I'm sure — not before!' he said.

'I call that mean . . . '

'You can call it what you like, darling! Now, let's talk about you, Mrs. Leyton . . . '

'Mrs. Heron has found me a job,' said Isobel. 'Isn't it wonderful?'

'That's fine! Where?'

'My hairdresser,' answered Thelma. 'He wanted a receptionist, I introduced him to Isobel, who was with me and — voila!'

'Pretty quick work!' said Heron.

'I've told her that she can stay here until she can find a flat,' said Thelma. 'And you can see about the divorce . . . '

'It's terribly kind of you both,' said the girl. 'It was lucky for me that I came down to Bishop's Trencham that night. I don't know what I should have done . . . '

'There's no need to worry about that now,' said Heron. 'We're only too glad to have been a bit helpful . . . '

'I can never thank you enough . . . '

'Don't try, dear,' said Thelma. 'What's the next move, Felix?'

'I shall return to Trencham Close first thing tomorrow morning.'

'I see.' Thelma pursed her lips. 'Have you any idea where the diamonds are hidden?'

Heron shook his head.

'Not the faintest!' he declared.

'They wouldn't take up much room, not ten stones.'

'No. They could be anywhere in the house, or they might not have been hidden in the house at all . . .'

'The secret must be in that book, Felix! Have you really examined it thoroughly?'

'There's absolutely nothing unusual about it.'

'Do you mind if I have another look?'

'Go ahead! If you can find anything I'll be surprised. I can't!'

He fetched the book and Thelma began to go through it page by page. Heron left them both with their heads together, bent over the printed pages, and went into the office to speak to Harry.

'I want you to see if you can find out anything concerning a man named James Wyseman, Harry,' he said. 'Here is his last address.' He laid down the paper on which he had scribbled the address Mr. Jacobs had given him. 'See if you can get the names of any friends who might have called to see him.'

'Okay,' said Harry. 'I'll go along now.'

'Make it quite a casual inquiry. If he isn't still there say you've lost touch with him while you were abroad, or something like that.'

'Leave it to me!' said Harry.

14

1

Harry stood on the narrow strip of pavement and eyed the house speculatively.

It was one of a row in a dingy street of terraced houses, all alike except for the curtains and the varying degrees of dirt and dilapidation.

Number Sixteen, the one he was interested in, was even dirtier and in a worse state of repair than its fellows. A flight of worn and broken steps led up to a front door that had once been green but was now, due to a combination of rain and sun, an almost indescribable colour. The steps were protected on one side by an iron rail and at the foot of each side was a broken urn that had, at one time, been the receptacle for flowers.

In the window of the lower bay was a notice that read simply 'Apartments.' The windows themselves were hung with lace curtains of a depressing greyness and marred by a number of large holes. In the centre of the middle window stood a wooden stand on which a wilting plant drooped unhappily in a china pot.

The whole house had about it an atmosphere of seediness, like a man who had failed and taken to drink in his old age.

Harry walked up the stone steps and knocked with the rusty and twisted iron knocker.

There was no reply and he knocked again. It was at the third attempt that he got an answer. A shuffling step reached his ears and the door was opened by a slatternly woman carrying a baby in her arms. She was a thin-faced woman with tired, red-rimmed eyes and straggling hair that fell partly over her eyes where it had escaped from a number of curlers that adorned her head. The baby began to cry as she peered out at Harry.

'I'm very sorry to trouble you,' he said, 'but . . .'

'Yer want a room?' she interrupted, and

gave the baby a little shake.

'Well, no . . . '

'If yer sellin' somethin' I don't want it,' she said. 'Be quiet, will yer?'

The baby instead of heeding this request only cried louder.

'For heavens sake, shut up!' said the woman crossly.

'I just want to ask you about a friend of mine,' said Harry. 'Is he in?'

'Who d'yer want?' she demanded.

'My friend's name is Wyseman, James Wyseman . . . '

''E ain't 'ere. 'E's left . . . '

She attempted to shut the door but Harry put his foot over the threshold.

'Left?' he said with an element of surprise in his voice. 'When did he leave?'

'Several weeks,' she answered.

'Can you tell me where he's gone?'

'Can't tell yer nothin' about 'im, mister,' she said. 'If yer don't shut up, I'll give yer a good wallopin'!'

The unfortunate baby uttered several loud yells and was immediately spanked which only had the effect of increasing the power of its lungs.

'I'm very anxious to find Mr. Wyseman,' said Harry. 'I've been abroad and lost touch with him . . . '

'I don't know nothin' about 'im, mister,' she snapped. 'He's gorn an' I don't know no more . . . '

Harry produced a pound note from his pocket and held it carelessly in his fingers. The woman's eyes fastened on it and her manner became less unpleasant.

'If I could 'elp yer, I would,' she began in a more conciliatory tone.

'Perhaps you could remember the names of any friends who may have called while he was staying here?' he suggested.

' 'E wasn't in much,' she replied. 'Jest 'ad 'is room an' breakfast. Got 'is other food out. I never see much of him . . . '

'He didn't owe you any rent, did he?'

He saw the struggle that went on in her mind but she resisted the temptation and shook her head. One of the curlers came loose and dropped on the floor. Harry stooped and picked it up.

'Oh, thanks!' She took the curler and pushed it into her pocket. 'Wish I could 'elp yer, mister . . . '

'Who is it? What's goin' on?' A rough, thick voice broke in on what she was saying. Behind her a man appeared at the other end of the passage. He was a small, unshaven man with a shock of closely cropped hair that grew down low on his narrow forehead. His shirt sleeves were rolled up above his elbows showing his thin but sinewy arms.

'It's all right, Bert . . . '

'What's this chap want then?' Bert came up behind the woman and stared at Harry suspiciously.

' 'E jest wanted to know about Mr. Wyseman . . . '

'Oh, did 'e? We don't know nothin' about 'im.'

'I've told 'im that . . . '

'No good talkin' any more then, is there? Come on. I want me grub . . . '

'I'm trying to trace my friend,' explained Harry. He repeated what he had told the woman, fingering the pound note ostentatiously. The man's eyes flickered greedily.

'Of course, if you can't help me . . . '

' 'Old on, mister,' broke in Bert as

Harry was about to turn away. 'I can tell yer the place Wyseman was goin' to, if that's any good to yer . . . '

'Do yer know, Bert?' asked the woman in surprise. 'Yer never said nuthink ter me.'

'Wasn't no reason, was there? 'E paid up before 'e went.'

'You know where Wyseman went from here?' asked Harry.

'That's right.' Bert nodded, his eyes still fixed on the pound note in the other's hand. 'Are yer offerin' that for the infermashun, mister?'

'If it's worth it.'

'Yer can judge for yerself. Yer friend was talkin' to a long-jawed chap on the step, 'ere, when I come 'ome. 'E was goin' the next day, yer see, an' I 'eard 'im say 'see yer in Bishop's Trencham' . . . '

Harry thrust the pound note into Bert's willing hand.

'Thanks,' he said. 'I won't trouble you any more.'

He looked back as he reached the bottom of the steps. The baby was yelling lustily while the woman argued shrilly with the man, Bert.

Harry guessed that they were disputing the rightful ownership of the pound note!

2

'That's the link,' said Felix Heron when Harry made his report. 'Wyseman was employed by Jacobs. He knew about the diamonds and soon after Sir Percival bought them, he left his job and went to Bishop's Trencham. It fits.'

'What about Drebner and Cripps?' asked Thelma.

'One step at a time,' answered Heron. 'I should say it was possible that the man he was talking to on the step when Bert saw them was Drebner. He said he was 'a long-jawed chap,' didn't he, Harry?'

Harry nodded.

'Wouldn't you describe Alfred Lessinger as long-jawed? And Drebner was very like Lessinger. I think we can assume that the man Wyseman was talking to was Drebner.'

'You're probably right, darling,' said Thelma. 'You nearly always are. But I'll tell you something. There's nothing in that book at all. Isobel and I have been through it from cover to cover. There's nothing — nothing at all!'

'You surprise me!' said Heron. 'After all that brain work you should have a good rest. I suggest an early night and we can leave for Bishop's Trencham first thing in the morning.'

A drizzle of rain was falling when they left London. Thin, spider-web clouds drifted across the sky in the dim light of a dull morning. The rain stopped when they were half-way on their journey, and the grey clouds frayed away like unravelled threads of gossamer until the sky was clear and a pale and watery sun struggled for life.

On the way to Trencham Close they stopped at the cottage hospital to inquire how Dick Farrell was. At that early hour they were not particularly popular. The matron informed them, rather acidly, that the reporter was a little better. He had recovered consciousness for a few minutes on the previous evening but his condition was still serious. He was on no account to be disturbed. The thing he needed most was sleep and rest — as much as possible. The injury to his head had been a severe one. There was no damage to the brain but it had received a shock which had been transmitted to the whole system.

'It will be several days before Mr. Farrell is quite recovered,' said the matron. 'During the next day or so I have orders to see that he is kept as quiet as possible.'

Charles Rayner was out when they reached the house. He was somewhere in the grounds with Thomas, the gardener, discussing repairs to some fencing, but Marian, who told them this, was in the drawing-room talking to Harry Glenn.

'Anything fresh?' asked Glenn. 'Did you find anything in the book?'

'There's absolutely nothing in the book!' declared Thelma. 'Isobel and I examined it thoroughly . . . '

'How is Isobel?' asked Marian.

'She's fine!' said Heron. He told them about the job that the girl had got, and Marian was delighted.

'You have been kind,' she said. 'I do hope that Isobel will find some real happiness now. She's had such a bad time, and she's so sweet.'

'She'll be all right,' said Heron. 'Nothing's been happening here, I suppose?'

Glenn shook his head.

'Quiet as a church,' he replied. 'No tramps, no murders, nothing!'

'A little monotonous, eh?'

'Oh, no! It's wonderful here — wonderful!' exclaimed Harry enthusiastically, and for some reason Marian's cheeks became a little pinker.

Heron raised one eyebrow.

'I see,' he remarked dryly. 'Well, you'd better make the most of the quiet spell. I've an idea that it's going to get pretty exciting in the next few hours.'

15

1

In spite of Felix Heron's prophecy the rest of the day passed peacefully enough. During lunch Heron told them of his visit to Mr. Jacobs but he did not mention James Wyseman or what his secretary had learned from Bert.

'Well, now we know for certain what's at the bottom of this business,' said Rayner. 'Trench hid those diamonds somewhere and these people are after them.'

'That book wouldn't have done them any good, even if they'd got hold of it,' said Thelma. 'I wonder why they thought it would?'

'They must have had a good reason,' said Heron.

'How did they know it existed?' asked Glenn.

Heron shook his head.

'I've no idea. Perhaps we shall find out when we get the people responsible for all this mayhem.'

'If we ever do!' grunted Rayner.

'We shall — maybe sooner than you think.'

Rayner shot Heron a quick glance.

'Got something up your sleeve, eh?'

Heron smiled.

'If I have, I'll keep it there — for the time being,' he said.

During the afternoon, Felix Heron sought out Stukes, the butler, and had a long conversation with the old man which seemed to astonish and worry him.

'Do it carefully,' said Heron. 'Don't make it at all blatant, will you?'

'I'll do my best, sir,' said Stukes.

Heron thanked him and went in search of Thelma.

'I'm going up to the cottage,' he informed her. 'I don't suppose I shall be very long.'

'You don't want me to come with you?'

He shook his head.

'No, you stay here. I shan't be more than an hour or two.'

He took the car and drove round as far as the lane. Here he left the car because he couldn't take it any further and climbed up the slope to the cottage.

Letting himself in he lit an oil stove — the place was very cold and damp — and sat down. After some time there was a knock on the front door. Heron opened it and admitted Waldron, his secretary, Harry, and the man named Bert.

'Well, here we are,' said Waldron. 'I hope the journey's going to be worth it!'

'So do I,' said Heron. 'Have you explained to this man what we want him to do?' He indicated Bert.

Harry nodded.

'It's a rum sort o' 'ow-d'ye-do, ain't it?' grunted Bert. 'Wot's it all abart?'

'Never mind that,' said Heron. 'You're being well paid.'

'Oh, I ain't grumblin', guv-nor . . . '

'Good!' said Heron. 'I'm going to leave you now. Here's the key of the cottage.' He tossed it over to Harry who caught it deftly. 'At nine o'clock I want you to flash a torch three times if everything's all right. I'll be on the look-out from

Trencham Close. If it's not all right
— one flash. Clear?'

'Quite clear,' said Harry.

'You know what to do after that,' said
Heron. 'Be very careful. We don't want to
scare our bird.'

'We'll do our part, don't worry,' said
Waldron.

'Right! Then make yourselves as
comfortable as possible. There's a good
part of a bottle of John Haig in the
cupboard and several bottles of beer. I'm
off! Keep sober!'

He grinned at them and hurried away
down the slope to his waiting car.

He said nothing about the presence of
the other three when he came into the
drawing-room.

'Hello,' greeted Glenn. 'Where have
you been?'

'Just getting a breath of fresh air,'
answer Heron.

'When does all the excitement start?'

'I can't tell you exactly. But you'll
know!'

'Felix loves keeping up the suspense,
don't you, darling?' said his wife.

224

'Crime is sordid and rather dull,' said Heron. 'I like to add a little spice, if possible.'

Stukes wheeled in a wagon of drinks. Catching Heron's eye he gave a barely perceptible nod.

Charles Rayner joined them as the butler began to arrange the glasses. He was glowing from the keen air and went over to the fire and warmed his hands.

'Been round with the gardener,' he said. 'Lot of work wants doing in the garden. Trench didn't bother much. Doubt if Thomas will be able to cope on his own . . . '

'Are you having the usual, sir?' asked Stukes.

'Whisky. Make it a stiff one! Jolly cold and damp trudging round this time of the year.'

The butler poured out a large John Haig and brought it over with a jug of water. Rayner added a little water and took a long drink.

'By jove, that's better,' he said. 'Where's Marian?'

'Miss Marian's upstairs in her room,

sir,' answered Stukes. He mixed a Gordon's pink gin for Heron and poured out a sherry for Thelma. He had just given them the drinks when Marian came in. She had changed her dress for a semi-evening gown and looked very attractive. Harry Glenn stood up as she came in and literally gaped, to the girl's evident amusement and, no doubt, secret satisfaction.

Stukes supplied her with a Dry Fly sherry and Harry with a gin and French and went silently out.

Dinner was a silent meal, interspersed by gusts of desultory conversation in which no one was interested. They were all suffering from suppressed excitement. Heron was the only one among them who seemed completely cool. He refused to be drawn. Having warded off all questions concerning the possible events of the night, he talked about everything except the case — when he talked at all.

At a few minutes before nine o'clock, he excused himself and went upstairs and into the room which had been Dick Farrell's. Going over to the window he gazed out into the darkness of the night.

It was very dark. There was no moon to offer even a modicum of light and the sky was overcast. It was exactly nine when a bright little spark flashed from the hillside. It was repeated three times. Heron expelled his breath with relief. It had turned out as he had hoped.

2

At eleven o'clock it started to rain. Low, leaden clouds scudded across the sky driven by a gusty wind which whistled through the trees and rustled the ivy that clung to the old walls of Trencham Close.

Down in the village the streets were deserted. The inhabitants of Bishop's Trencham retired early and not even a light showed from any window.

But there was one wakeful person that night.

With the collar of his coat pulled close round his neck, a man came quickly along the High Street, his hands thrust deep into the pockets of his streaming raincoat.

He came to the drive leading up to Trencham Close, turned in through the gates, and melted into the shadows.

Keeping on the strip of grass that bordered the gravel, he advanced towards the house. As he rounded the bend he saw that it, like the houses in the village, was in darkness.

Cautiously he found his way round the angle of the house and came to the back door. Gently he tapped and the door was instantly opened. It remained open long enough for him to slip within and then it was shut behind him. A hand gripped his arm in the complete darkness and a voice whispered in his ear. He was led gently into the great kitchen, along the passage, and up into the hall. The darkness had gathered in the deep shadows by the massive staircase, and into this black pool, the newcomer and his guide vanished from sight.

Complete silence hung heavily in the air inside Trencham Close, an unbroken silence that seemed to be thick and tangible.

And yet, not all the inmates of the

house were sleeping. There were shadows in the library — dark shadows that moved without sound — as the clock on the carved mantelpiece struck twelve. The bell shattered the silence like a stone breaking a pane of glass, and then, as the last stroke faded away, the silence flooded back once more like a thick, oozing tide.

The hiss of the rain against the windows changed to a sound like thousands of tiny fingers tapping for admission as it began to fall more heavily.

Half an hour passed and from the back of the house came a sharp sound — a click followed by the creak of a raised window. Coincident with it there was a gentle tapping on the library window from outside. There was no answer from within and the tapping was not repeated.

A faint spark of light flickered in the darkness of the hall. It wavered and moved from side to side, the dim glow from a torch, masked so that only a pin-point of light escaped from the lens. The man who held the torch, a muffled figure in an overcoat, moved very cautiously towards the library door.

Reaching it, he softly turned the handle and opened the door. Slipping inside he closed the door behind him and paused. The tiny light of the torch danced around the big room and flickered across the picture of the man in lace and ruffles with his perpetual sneering smile, and then focussed on the rows of bookshelves. Back and forth it swept from shelf to shelf, pausing for a moment now and again, and sweeping on again.

At last it stopped, pin-pointing one particular volume. A gloved hand stretched out and reached up, grasping the book and pulling it from the shelf.

And at the same instant the centre lights in the big room blazed to life!

The intruder, the book still in his hand, whirled round with a sharp exclamation — and faced Felix Heron as he emerged from behind the curtains at the windows. He held an automatic in his hand.

'Don't move!' he said curtly. 'Waldron!'

Detective Chief Superintendent Waldron straightened up from behind the back of one of the big easy chairs.

'Run through his pockets,' said Heron.

Waldron went over and ran his hands expertly over the startled man. He found a small pistol which he held up.

'That's all,' he said.

'It's enough,' said Heron. 'That's James Wyseman, the murderer of George Mellins and Michael Drebner. Ring Trafford, will you? I'd like to get this beauty under lock and key. He's dangerous!'

As Waldron picked up the receiver, Charles Rayner appeared in the doorway.

'What's going on?' he demanded. 'I heard a noise and came to see what was happening . . . '

'We've caught the man responsible for all the trouble,' said Felix Heron. 'Take a good look at him!'

Rayner came quickly forward and the cornered man turned a hate-distorted face towards him.

'Good God!' exclaimed Rayner, staring. 'That's my gardener!'

16

1

In the early hours of the morning the household at Trencham Close gathered round the drawing-room fire and drank hot coffee which a hastily aroused Stukes had prepared for them.

Inspector Trafford, wakened from his sleep, had arrived in answer to Waldron's telephone call and listened in astonishment to what they had to tell him. At first he refused to believe it. But the evidence of Bert, who had identified Thomas, the gardener, as James Wyseman, his wife's erstwhile lodger was irrefutable. This, coupled with the fact that Wyseman had been caught with the book actually in his hand and that he had also broken into the house by forcing open a back window, convinced Trafford in spite of himself.

Wyseman, sullen and tight-lipped, refused to make any statement at all, and was taken away by Trafford and Waldron to be charged and locked up in the single cell which Bishop Trencham police station boasted.

'I can scarcely believe it,' said Charles Rayner, shaking his head. 'How did you spot that it was Thomas?'

'I didn't actually know that Thomas was Wyseman until Bert identified him,' said Heron. 'But when I first saw your gardener he was wearing one of those short leather jackets with a fur collar. In the kitchen of the house where they took Marian, I found some hairs that looked as if they came from that collar . . . '

'And that made you suspicious of Thomas?'

'Well, it was a pointer in that direction. Of course I knew nothing about Wyseman at that time but when I learned about him from Jacobs, and later heard from Bert that he'd been talking to a man who answered to the description of Drebner and that he'd mentioned Bishop's Trencham I began to put two and two together. I didn't know about Bert when I faked that book . . . '

'Are you telling me,' exclaimed Thelma, 'that the book you found wasn't the real book?'

'Of course, it wasn't! I bought a copy of *The Sinister Man* and stuck it in the cover of *Pope's Essays* . . . '

'You let Isobel and me spend all that time trying to find out the secret . . . '

'You were so keen, darling,' said Heron, 'I hadn't the heart to stop you!'

'Pig!' His wife very rudely stuck her tongue out at him.

'I still don't understand,' broke in Rayner. 'How do all these other people come into it — the man who was hanged on that tree, Drebner, this chap Cripps . . . '

'I'm hoping that we shall learn a lot from Cripps,' said Heron. 'He was arrested earlier last night at Basingstoke just as he was getting on the London train.'

'But,' Rayner was still puzzled. 'Why go to all that trouble over the book . . . ?'

'It was the cheese to get the rat into the trap,' explained Felix. 'Even with the identification by Bert, which I didn't know about at that time, there wasn't enough evidence to connect Wyseman with this business. A clever lawyer could have made rings round the prosecution. Why shouldn't he have taken a job with Sir Percival as a gardener? Perhaps, he didn't want his friends to know that he was doing a menial job? So he didn't use his own name. We know why he took the job, because he was after those diamonds. But if he was caught with the book actually in his hand *after* Bert had identified him as Wyseman, we had him really tied up . . . '

'How did he know about the book?'

'I took care of that. I arranged with Stukes to spread the news among the servants and to see that it particularly reached Thomas. Also that I considered that the best hiding-place was among the other books in the library . . . '

'Wyseman fell for it?'

'He did. Waldron and I were waiting for him in the library . . . '

'And the real book has still to be found?' asked Thelma.

'That's right,' agreed Heron.

'And the diamonds.'

'Yes. We've got the man but there's still a lot to be done before we can write 'finis' to this business.'

Although Wyseman refused to talk, Stephen Cripps was made of less obstinate material. Chief Superintendent Waldron came back during the morning with a copy of the statement he had made. James Wyseman, who had had two convictions against him for petty theft, had first heard of the diamonds when Sir Percival Trench had been discussing the purchase with Jacobs. He obtained a job with Trench as gardener at once in the hope of being able to get hold of the diamonds. But he could discover nothing concerning their whereabouts, although he was convinced that they were somewhere concealed in Trencham Close.

He had come to the conclusion that the only way to find them was to force Sir Percival to reveal what he had done with them. Accident played into his hands in more ways than one. He was out for a walk when he had seen Trench cantering across a meadow, having become detached from the main hunt. Almost at the moment that he saw him, the horse had stumbled and thrown its rider. Wyseman ran to his employer's assistance and found that Sir Percival had broken his neck in the fall.

It struck Wyseman that here was his chance to find a clue to the hiding place of the diamonds. He searched the dead man's pockets and found a small notebook. He didn't wait to go through it then in case some member of the hunt should come back and see him. He took it to the little room over the stables which had been given him to live in. Here he examined it carefully.

To his disappointment there was nothing about the diamonds. But there was one entry that might refer to what he was seeking. It ran 'See 'The Sinister Man'.' Wyseman knew that Edgar Wallace had written a book with this title — in fact he had read it. He concluded that the secret of the hiding-place was to be found in this book. But, although he searched the house, he couldn't find it.

It was at this period that Michael Drebner put in an appearance. He had been puzzled why Wyseman should have gone to a small village like Bishop's Trencham and was even more puzzled when he found him masquerading as a gardener. Wyseman was glad to have an accomplice to help him. He told Drebner the story of the diamonds and agreed to split the proceeds with him. He had seen Lessinger and was struck by the resemblance he bore to Drebner. The likeness might be used to advantage. He arranged for Drebner to disguise himself as a tramp and keep an eye on the house when he, Wyseman, was unable to. Drebner let his beard grow, dressed in ragged clothes, and camped out near Denham Wood.

Drebner was willing to fall in with Wyseman's plans up to a point. But he had no intention of sharing the diamonds once they were found. He was determined to get them for himself.

And then George Mellins took a hand in the game. He had been interested in Drebner for some time. The man was a known crook and Mellins, always curious, wanted to know what he was up to. He came down to the village and discovered Drebner in his guise of a tramp. He overheard a conversation between Drebner and Wyseman which told him the reason they were there. Foreseeing that he could make more out of this situation by joining them than by acting in his usual capacity as a 'grass' he tackled Wyseman, demanded a lump sum of money to keep his mouth shut.

Wyseman had agreed, but he had no intention of paying. He asked Mellins to wait while he raised the money. Mellins was willing to wait for a little while. He joined Drebner at the camp near Denham Wood. Two tramps, very much alike in appearance, were unlikely to attract much attention. But Wyseman, in order to alibi himself in case he needed one, drew the attention of the household to the presence of the tramps, while he planned to get rid of Mellins.

Meanwhile, Drebner, hoping to get ahead of his partner, kidnapped Marian Rayner. Wyseman was furious when he heard about it, but pretended to agree after an argument with Drebner at the old cottage to which the latter had taken the girl. It was a coincidence that Drebner should have chosen to kidnap the girl on the same night that Wyseman had planned to get rid of Mellins which he had done by arranging to meet him at the tree to hand over the money Mellins had demanded. Wyseman had got there prior to the appointment, climbed the tree and lain along the branch with the noosed rope ready. When Mellins arrived he dropped the noose over his head as he stood beneath the tree, jumped down with the rope in his hand, which he had looped over a branch, and tied it to the trunk.

This had disposed of Mellins but Wyseman did not know that he had been working in conjunction with his pal, Cripps. When Cripps heard of the murder of Mellins he knew who was responsible and came down to Bishop's Trencham. He was puzzled and suspicious when he had run into Lessinger in the High Street immediately on his arrival. He thought it was Drebner, and wondered why the man denied the fact.

Cripps got in touch with Wyseman and demanded a meeting. He took the precaution of telling Wyseman that he had left an account of what he knew with a friend who would go to the police if anything happened to him. He knew nothing at this period about Drebner's death but enough concerning the death of Mellins and the rest of it to demand a share in the diamonds.

Wyseman, dismayed at this new danger, met him at the milestone and they were discussing the situation when they became aware that Dick Farrell was listening. Cripps had struck at Farrell with the intention of knocking him out, but Wyseman had shot him. They had pulled the body into the wood believing that Farrell was dead.

Cripps had been thoroughly scared. He was not used to violence and didn't want to get mixed up with it. He fled back to his lodgings, deciding to leave the whole thing alone and go back to London. It was while he was waiting for his train at Basingstoke that he had been picked up by the police.

'That's a pretty clear statement,' said

Waldron. 'Apparently, Mellins kept him well-informed by phone how things were going so he knew all about it . . . '

'And what he didn't know he guessed, eh?' said Heron. 'Still it certainly clears up quite a lot. It seems pretty obvious now why Drebner was shot. Wyseman knew the book hadn't been found but he didn't tell Drebner. He arranged for the man to come and collect it so that he could get rid of him with very little risk to himself.'

'And Drebner shaved off his tramp's beard so that if he were seen he'd be mistaken for Lessinger?' said the Chief Superintendent.

'That's about it. I've found the boots Wyseman wore in his room. They fit the footprints left by the murderer. Danger-ous fellow, James Wyseman!'

'He won't be dangerous any more,' grunted Waldron.

'He could be!' said Heron. 'In the days when murderers were hanged, he'd have been a danger to society no longer. But, now that capital punishment has been abolished, there's nothing to prevent him committing a few more murders when he's released after his sentence.'

'I couldn't agree with you more.'

'The victims, of course, don't count. They're dead. No consideration can be given to them. But at least their deaths can be avenged and any possible future victims be safeguarded. These half-baked idealists who want to cosset the criminal are almost as big a menace to society as he is.'

'Nothing can be done about it, unfortunately,' said Waldron. 'We've done our part, anyway. We've caught Wyseman . . . '

'And we've still got to find the diamonds,' interrupted Heron. 'Until that's done I don't feel that I've really completed the job.'

It was many days later that he found the hiding-place and then it was due to a chance remark made by somebody whom he had never seen before in his life.

17

1

Dick Farrell was convalescent and back at Trencham Close. James Wyseman had been removed to London after being committed for trial by the magistrates at Basingstoke. At the urgent request of Charles Rayner, Felix Heron and his wife had agreed to stay at Trencham Close for a few days holiday.

Heron was only too pleased to accept the invitation because it gave him a further opportunity to find the hiding-place of the diamonds. His failure to do so rankled and he was determined to succeed. But everything he tried met with failure.

'Perhaps Sir Percival didn't hide them in the house, after all,' said Thelma. 'Actually there's no proof that he did, is there?'

'No, but I've got a feeling that he did.'

'They wouldn't take up much room. They could be anywhere.'

'I know,' said Heron irritably. 'You don't have to tell me.'

'Short of pulling the place down brick by brick, I don't see how you're going to find them. The book is a wash out — not the one you faked — but the one you *thought* existed . . . '

'What about that entry in the note-book?'

'The one Wyseman took from Sir Percival's dead body?'

'Yes.'

'Well, the book isn't to be found, is it?'

'It could be somewhere. Supposing somebody borrowed it and hasn't returned it . . . '

'Don't be silly, darling! If it contained the secret of the hiding-place would Trench be such a lunatic as to lend it to anyone?'

'It might not have been Trench.'

'What do you mean?'

'Books have been borrowed without asking. One of the servants who were here at the time might have borrowed it.'

'In that case I don't see how you are ever going to find it.'

'Neither do I at the moment.'

Thelma finished brushing her hair and got up from the dressing-table. She slipped out of her dressing-gown and got into bed. They were talking in their bedroom at Trencham Close preparatory to going to bed.

'Supposing we never find those diamonds?' asked his wife, sitting up in bed and clasping her knees. 'Supposing they're never found?'

Heron shrugged his shoulders.

'We can only do our best,' he said. 'I hate to leave a job in the air, and this won't be really finished until those diamonds are found.'

He slept badly, his mind going over and over the problem of the diamonds and wondering if there was any possibility he had overlooked. Thelma was sleeping peacefully beside him, breathing softly and regularly, and he envied her. At last he did fall asleep but it was a fitful sleep that was troubled with disjointed dreams, absurd dreams without any beginning or end, in which showers of diamonds poured out of the mouth of a grotesque gargoyle perched on the top of a chimney stack on the roof of Trencham Close.

When he came down to breakfast on the following morning he felt tired and jaded.

'You look as if you'd had a bad night,' said Rayner, helping himself to kidneys and bacon from the dish on the sideboard.

'I did!'

They were the first down.

'Why?' asked his host, bringing his plate over to the table and pouring himself a cup of coffee.

'I was thinking about those infernal diamonds.'

'I should give up worrying about them. It's my opinion they'll never be found. I don't believe Trench hid them here at all. Probably deposited them in a safe deposit somewhere . . . '

Heron shook his head. He helped himself to some coffee and a piece of toast.

'I'm quite sure he didn't,' he replied,

reaching for the butter and buttering his toast. 'He put those diamonds somewhere readily accessible . . . '

He stopped as Harry Glenn came into the dining-room.

'Hello,' he greeted. 'Where's Marian?'

'Not down yet,' grunted Rayner. 'There's kidneys and bacon, kippers, or cold ham. Help yourself.'

Glenn went over to the sideboard and inspected the contents of the hotplates. He decided on kippers and carried his plate back to the table.

'By the way,' remarked Rayner, as Glenn sat down beside Heron, 'you must meet Hanbury. He's a very nice chap . . . '

'Who is he?'

'He's the vicar — great friend of Trench's, incidentally, or rather was. He's been away or you'd have met him before. He's coming over to tea.'

'Friend of Trench's, was he? How friendly were they?'

'Thick as thieves, I believe,' answered Rayner. 'Used to play chess together. Pass the toast, will you?'

Heron complied.

'Maybe he can help us,' he said.

'About the diamonds?' Rayner shook his head. 'I should imagine if Trench had told anyone it would have been Miss Lessinger. Still he might be able to suggest something.'

Heron, who had reached the stage when he was prepared to clutch at any straw, sincerely hoped that he would.

2

The Reverend Michael Hanbury was a bluff, stout, hearty man. He was short and his lack of inches made him seem fatter than he really was. His face was ruddy and his eyes, small and bright, twinkled with the joy of life.

Tea was served in the drawing-room, presided over by Marian, who obviously liked the vicar very much. Harry Glenn sat in silence, glowering, while the Reverend Hanbury chattered on incessantly, laughing heartily at his own jokes.

He was very disappointed that he had been away during all the excitement.

'I read all about it in the newspapers, of course,' he said. 'Poor old Trench! He'd have had a fit if he'd known what his queer ideas would lead to. Of course, I'd no inkling that he'd carried them to the lengths of converting his entire fortune into diamonds.'

'He didn't tell you?' asked Heron.

'Good gracious, no!' answered the Reverend Hanbury, shaking his head and helping himself to another hot buttered scone — his fifth. 'I should have done my best to dissuade him if he had. What did he do with these stones?'

'That's what we'd like to know.'

'You haven't found them?'

'No,' answered Heron. 'If we could find the book we might . . . '

The vicar's twinkling eyes surveyed him questioningly.

'What book is this?' he asked.

'He mentioned it in his diary,' explained Heron. '*The Sinister Man* . . . '

Mr. Hanbury's fat, genial face twitched and he broke into a throaty chuckle. The chuckle developed into a gust of laughter and his entire body shook with mirth.

They looked at him in astonishment. The tears were streaming down his red cheeks and he gasped for breath.

'What the deuce is so amusing, Hanbury?' demanded Rayner.

The vicar took out his handkerchief and wiped his eyes.

'Excuse me,' he panted. 'It struck me as funny! You thought it was a book, did you?'

'Isn't it?' asked Heron.

The vicar shook his head, striving to regain his composure.

'No, I'm sure it wasn't. You see Trench always referred to the picture as 'The Sinister Man.' It was his nickname for it . . . '

'Do you mean the painting in the library?'

'Yes, the chap in the ruffles and lace . . . '

Heron jumped to his feet.

'What an idiot I am!' he exclaimed. 'Why didn't I think of that. Come on, we'll follow this up at once!'

They followed him into the library. The painting of the man in lace and ruffles sneered down at them from its golden frame. The lips were curled in a one-sided smile, the eyes, narrowed and hard, stared with a cruel glint in their depths.

The Sinister Man!

Now that he had been given the clue, Heron wondered how on earth he had come to miss something so obvious. It fitted so perfectly! Sinister was the description that most sprang to the mind!

And yet he had missed it!

Heron dragged a chair over and, climbing on it, examined the painting more closely. It hung from two chains attached to hooks on the picture-rail. He tried to lift it but it was too heavy.

'Give me a hand, will you?' he asked.

'There's a pair of library steps over here,' said Rayner. 'I'll bring them.'

He wheeled them over to the fireplace and between them, assisted by Harry Glenn, they succeeded in lifting the painting down. Carrying it over to the big table they laid it down carefully.

'There's something on the back,' said Thelma. 'I saw it when you were getting it down. Something white.'

They turned the heavy painting over. On the back of the canvas was a rough drawing in what appeared to be white chalk.

'It's a plan of the rose garden,' said Heron. 'Look. There's the sundial . . . '

'And it's marked with a cross!' broke in his wife excitedly.

'Does that mean the diamonds are hidden in the sundial?' asked Marian.

'Yes, I think we've found them,' said Heron.

'Let's go and look,' said Marian. 'Come on, Harry!'

'Wait a minute!' said Heron. 'We've got to do this methodically.'

'What's all the rumpus?' broke in a voice from the door. Dick Farrell, his head still bandaged and wearing a dressing-gown, came in a little unsteadily.

'You shouldn't have got up, Farrell,' said Heron.

'What's happening?' demanded Dick.

Heron explained.

'Now, you sit down and wait until we come back,' he ended. 'The doctor said you were to stay in bed for at least another three days . . . '

'I'm not going to be left out of this,' broke in Dick. 'I'm coming with you . . . '

'Don't be silly,' said Thelma. 'You can't come out like that. You'll catch your death of cold . . . '

'I'll put a coat on . . . '

'You'll sit here,' said Heron firmly. 'Don't argue! We'll tell you all about it when we come back.'

Dick grumbled but he agreed reluctantly.

They left him and went out into the hall. Going out by the front door they trooped round into the rose garden. The light was fading but there was still enough left for them to see.

'Where do you think he put them?' asked Glenn, as they gathered round the sundial.

'The most likely place would be under the metal plate holding the gnomon,' replied Heron. He examined the dial-plate. It seemed to fit fairly tightly into its bed of stone, but the cement round the edges, although discoloured, appeared fresher than it should have looked.

'We'll need a hammer and a chisel . . . '

'There're tools in the garage,' interrupted Rayner. 'I'll get them.'

He hurried away. While he was gone, Heron took a penknife from his pocket and scraped at the cement. It was hard but under the weather-staining looked new.

'I think this is it,' said Heron. 'Keep your fingers crossed!'

When Rayner returned with the tools, he carefully chipped round the metal dial. It took some time but at length he was able to prise the plate up. It was a heavy plate of copper but with an effort he lifted it free of its stone bed.

The others crowded round him and peered into the space that was revealed. A square cavity had been chipped out of the stone and in it, fitting snugly, was a metal box.

Heron lifted it out.

'We'll open it in the library,' he said. 'It's too dark out here.'

He put back the copper dial and they all hurried back to the house.

In the library, with Dick Farrell an

interested spectator, Felix Heron opened the box.

Nestling in velvet, flashing fire in sparks of red and green, orange and lilac from their facets, were ten of the most beautiful diamonds they had ever seen.

3

It was several months later. The cold of the winter was giving place to the warmth of spring. The distant cousin of Sir Percival Trench, to his surprise and delight, had heard the news of the discovery of the diamonds from Mr. Sedman and discovered that he was suddenly rich.

Felix Heron had almost forgotten the whole business when he received a card one morning, grinned as he saw what it was, and took it into Thelma.

'Do you want to go to a wedding?' he asked.

'Whose?' she demanded.

'Harry Glenn is getting married to Marian Rayner,' said her husband. 'We've been invited.'

'Let's go,' said Thelma. 'It's a long time since I've been to a wedding. I like to see some other poor woman caught in the spider's web — like I was!'

'Not a very good analogy,' retorted her husband. 'The female spider always eats her mate!'

THE END

We do hope that you have enjoyed reading this large print book.

Did you know that all of our titles are available for purchase?

We publish a wide range of high quality large print books including:
Romances, Mysteries, Classics
General Fiction
Non Fiction and Westerns

Special interest titles available in large print are:
The Little Oxford Dictionary
Music Book, Song Book
Hymn Book, Service Book

Also available from us courtesy of Oxford University Press:
Young Readers' Dictionary
(large print edition)
Young Readers' Thesaurus
(large print edition)

For further information or a free brochure, please contact us at:
Ulverscroft Large Print Books Ltd.,
The Green, Bradgate Road, Anstey,
Leicester, LE7 7FU, England.
Tel: (00 44) **0116 236 4325**
Fax: (00 44) **0116 234 0205**